A HOOD LOVE LIKE NO OTHER

NIKKI BROWN

SUPREME WORKS PUBLICATIONS

LAURENCE "LALA" MARKS

"Got damn it!" I yelled as I flicked the light switch on and off with no results. "I knew I should have paid it myself." I was kicking myself for giving my mother the money to pay the light bill. Cynthia Marks wasn't the most reliable person, especially when it came to handling money. She was a stone-cold alcoholic, and me giving her money to take care of the bills that she refused to pay, was a lapse in judgment on my part. "I can't wait to get out of here!" I yelled.

Things like this had been happening since my father was gunned down in front of us on my fourteenth birthday. Every-thing that I loved and cherished was gone in the blink of an eye on that day. Every year on my birthday, I was reminded of the day my world was crushed.

My dad was our everything. He made sure that me and my mother didn't want for anything. When he was alive, my world was alright. I was the only child and his pride and joy; he never went a day without letting me know that. *God, I missed my daddy.*

I was my dad's namesake, you could say. He wanted his first-born, whether boy or girl, to have his name. Lawrence Marks was a powerful name where we were from, so to carry that name was an honor. I was thankful he gave a feminine spin on it though.

When Dad died, it was like someone sucked the air out of my mother because she stopped caring about everything, including me. All her love and attention went to the bottle, where she found her peace, and I suffered as a result of it.

At the tender age of fourteen, I had taken on the task of taking care of myself and her. If it weren't for my best friend, Heart, I didn't know where I would be. He made sure I was straight, no matter what, especially when my mother went on her week-long drinking binges and left me to fend for myself. I resented her so much for checking out on me, but I loved her too; she was my mom.

"Mom!" I yelled, walking into her room. The stench of liquor burned my nostrils, mixed with the smell of ass because she failed to keep her hygiene up, especially when she was on her binges. "Why in the hell didn't you pay the fucking light bill!"

I had lost respect for her a long time ago, and I didn't feel the need to watch what I said or how I said it. When she turned her back on me for her own selfish reasons, I felt no need to treat her like my mother. She forgot who she was supposed to be for me, and I wasn't inclined to remind her.

"What in the hell you in here yelling for, lil' girl? Better take ya little nappy headed ass on somewhere now."

"No, Cynt!" I yelled, calling her by her name. "I gave you the money for the lights, so why are they off?"

"You ain't give me shit," she slurred. I looked around the room, and it was just nasty. I had just cleaned it up last week, and I wasn't about to do it again. Especially since she didn't appreciate it.

"You know I did. I don't make that much at Walmart, damn. The least you can do is pay the bill when it's due."

"Tell that little nappy headed boy to give you the money," she said, referring to Heart.

She stayed calling someone nappy headed when her hair was always standing up like a chicken. I remember people picking on me in high school, so I gave her the money to get it done for my graduation. In good ol' Cynthia fashion, she not only showed up with her hair still all over her head, she was drunk and belligerent along with that.

"I shouldn't have to ask him for anything when I gave you the damn money!" I screamed.

"You better watch yo' tone, Laurence. Yo' ass gon' respect me." She tried to get up off the bed and ended up falling on the floor. My eyes traced her frail body, and I couldn't do anything other than shake my head. And to think that my mother used to be one of the most beautiful women to ever walk the streets of Mooresville.

"This is what you want me to respect? Can't stay fucking

sober enough to pay the got damn light bill." I looked down at her dingy white shirt and the three-day old navy-blue joggers.

I swear I had never seen liquor do to anyone what it was doing to my mom. You would think that she was on drugs, but she wasn't; it was all booze—one reason I didn't fuck with it like that. I'd have a drink here and there but my high of choice was weed and even with that I watched my intake. I never wanted to be like her.

"You should be ashamed of yourself." I stepped over her and headed out the door, heading to the only person that I knew that I could go to. I hated to ask him. He was helping me enough, but I knew that he would do whatever he needed to do to make sure that I was okay. He hated my mother, but he helped out with bills for me.

Walking into the busy breezeway of the building I stayed in, there was never a dull moment in Kings Creek Apartments. I looked at all the kids running around cussing and being disrespectful, the local trap boys on the green box selling to the numerous fiends that plagued the projects, and the women dressed in little of nothing trying to catch their next come up. Oh the joys of living in the hood.

I swear I couldn't wait to get the hell out of here. Heart was helping put me through school. I couldn't get financial aid on my own, and my sorry excuse for a mother was too busy chugging down her next bottle to care about anything that had to do with me.

I really missed my dad. If he was here, he would never let her be like this. I remember when I would come home from school and have fresh baked cookies and shit like that. Now I came home to a smoky kitchen because she passed out with the stove on. I hated her and loved her at the same time.

"What's up, baby girl?" Heart said as soon as he saw me walk up to the green box. The green box was where all the local trap boys hung out waiting on their next lick. I couldn't help the smirk that formed on my lips as I watched him hugged up with the whore of the hood, Quinia. Her thirsty ass wasn't even on his level. I didn't know why his ass stayed leading her on.

"Can I talk to you for a minute?" I asked, and the bitch on his lap had the nerve to smack her lips. I was about to correct her, but Heart took care of that for me.

"You can get the hell on if you want to." He glared at her. "You already know what the deal is."

Everyone knew that when it came to me, Heart had me no matter what. He would literally drop whatever or whoever he was doing at the time for me. People would swear that we were more than just friends, but that's all that we were; his choice, not mine.

The conversation came up one night we were chilling and drinking, but he told me that he was no good for me; that he loved and respected me too much to fuck up my life. I respected him for that. But I was a big girl; I could take care of myself. Yet, for now, this was what it was.

Heart was five years older than me, and he ran the Kings Creek projects. Nothing came in or out of here without his knowledge. If you were anybody in Mooresville, you knew who Heart was.

Heart was a heartless son of a bitch in the streets, but with me, he was the sweetest most caring person in the world, which was why I wanted so much more than a friendship from him. In my heart of hearts, I believed that this man was made for me, and I had faith that our time was coming. But for now, I had to force myself to sit back and watch him with these girls.

"What's up, baby girl? You good?" He looked at me trying to figure out what was wrong with me. He could always tell when I wasn't my best; our chemistry was just that good.

"It's personal." I tilted my head to the side, further pissing off the Quinia bitch, but I wasn't about to talk about my issues in front of her, and he knew that. She was just mad because she knew she would never be what she wanted to be in his life, and I was the reason why.

"Aight. Come on." He tilted his head toward his apartment.

I smiled and waved at everybody while I followed him into the building that was at the very bottom of the projects. I walked into his apartment and sat down on the couch. The way he moved around made me fantasize about the things he could do to me. His caramel colored skin and the many tattoos that donned it brought out his thuggish appearance, and his bowed legs made him sexy.

"The fuck you looking all crazy for?" He snapped me out of my nasty thoughts of him, and I looked up into his eyes. His eyelashes were long just like a girl, and it made him look softer than he was. He hated for anyone to comment on them, but I loved them and did it anyway.

"Mom blew the light bill money again." My eyes left his, and

I tried to focus on anything but him at the moment because I knew that he was about to flip the hell out. He told me a long time ago to stop giving her money and just do it myself, but I didn't listen.

"Are you fucking serious, Lala?" I could hear the anger in his voice without even looking at him.

"Yeah. I gave her the money last week when I got paid." I cut my eyes in his direction, and he lowered his head and shook it. I knew he was mad, but there was nothing that we could do about it now; the deed was done.

"Why you didn't do that shit yourself? You know she ain't shit." His voice was calm, but I could hear the disappointment in his words.

"I know." I put my head down, but he walked over and lifted it back up by my chin. He searched my eyes before he released my chin and stuck his hand in his pocket.

"How much?"

"Two hundred and nine dollars."

"Here..." He pulled out a wad of money and started to count it off but then folded it back up and handed me the whole wad.

"This is too much, Heart."

"Don't start that shit, La. Go put that shit in the bank just in case something like this happens again and you need it."

I didn't bother to argue because it was no use. He did shit like this all the time, and it was one of the many reasons why I loved him. I appreciated him so much, but I didn't want him to think that he had to take care of me. He was already putting me through school. He would have a fit if I objected any of his help though.

"There go the keys to the Chevy." He pointed to the counter. "Go do what you gotta do. I'll see you when you get back," he said, heading to the back of the apartment. Before he made it to the back, there was a knock at the door. "The fuck is it?"

"It's me!" Quinia sounded aggravated, and that was funny to me.

Heart snatched the door open and just sat there and stared at her. She didn't say anything, and neither did he. She looked over at me and rolled her eyes, causing me to snicker.

"What's up?" he asked unenthusiastically.

"I thought we were chilling today," she whined, putting her hands on her shapely hips.

"Chill, yo. I'm coming back out." He tugged on the rim of his hat. "Yo' ass just in here being fucking nosy. What I got going on with La is none of your concern, but if you must know." He stopped and looked at me. "You will never be to me what she is. You can still suck my dick though." He shrugged his shoulders, and I laughed.

"I don't see anything funny." She glared at me and snaked her neck.

"I do, but I got shit to do." I stood up from the couch and headed toward the door, but Heart stopped me and kissed me. That was nothing out of the normal because we kissed all the time; nothing sexual but a peck on the lip when we were leaving each other or stuff like that. This time, I knew that he did it to piss her off, and it worked because she tried to push me, but he caught her arm.

"Don't get fucked up." He lightly pushed her back so that I could leave.

I didn't bother getting into it with his women because I knew my position in his life. Although I wanted it to be more, I was still more than they would ever be. I could handle my own, but I never had to when it came to the jealous bitches he dealt with. "I'll see you when you get back. Aye, and don't wreck my shit."

"Ain't nobody gon' do nothing to your car, boy."

"Yeah, and last time my shit came back with a scratch on the bumper." I laughed because I forgot I backed into the light pole. 'Til this day, I'd never told him the truth about that.

"I have no idea what you're talking about." We both laughed, and I walked out of the apartment. Quinia looked like she could take my head off. I could hear her questioning him, but that didn't have anything to do with me. That was just my best friend.

HEART QUAMERE STRONG

I hated to see Lala keep going through this shit. Her mother wasn't shit and hadn't been since Big L died. That shit was hard on everybody, but she took it to the extreme. She turned to the bottle and treated La like she didn't exist. La tried so hard to stay above water, but it was hard when you had someone constantly trying to drown you.

I was proud of her. She wasn't like these other bird brain ass girls, like the one that was standing in front of me waiting on an explanation that she was never gonna get. La was in college. I was helping her through nursing school. I had so much faith in her, and I would do anything to see her win.

Lala was the kind of woman that you locked down and committed to. As bad as I wanted that, I just couldn't do that to her. I knew who I was, and I was okay with it, but I knew that she needed more; she deserved more. I vowed to always be there for her, but that was as far as it went though.

I didn't know how to love her the way that she needed to be loved. No one ever showed me any, so I didn't know shit about it. I grew up in the foster care system. I never met my moms, or anyone that I was kin to biologically for that matter. She threw my ass away the very first time she saw me, just like every foster family I was with, so my attitude had been fuck it ever since.

The only thing my mother ever gave me was my name. I never knew why or the meaning behind it, and that fucked with me sometimes. Who would name their child Heart? I bet she didn't know that I would grow up to not have one, except when it came to Lala. She was the only one that lived there and probably would always be.

"Are you going to answer me, Heart? Why do you always diss me for her?"

"Because unlike you, she means something to me." My eyes bore through hers. I wanted to make sure that she knew that I meant everything that I said.

I couldn't count on my hands how many times we'd had this conversation. I guess since she'd been around the longest out of all the bitches I fucked with, she felt like she deserved some kind of special treatment that she would never get.

"You're fucking her, aren't you?"

I laughed. "Again, unlike you, she don't gotta fuck for a title." I headed toward my kitchen to grab a Coors because she was blowing my high. "You ain't even my girl. We just fuck from time to time, so you can dead all this questioning shit."

"Yeah, but I'm trying to be more." She placed her hand on my chest. I never understood why she kept putting herself out there for me. I never gave her any indication that she was anything more than a nut, but here she was.

"You know what you can be for me?" I leaned down and placed my lips to her ear. The smile that spread across her face was amusing. She just knew that I was about to tell her something sweet, but she should've known better. "A stress reliever." If looks could kill, I would be lying on somebody's cold slab right now. She rolled her eyes, smacked her lips, and crossed her arms across her chest. "Then get the fuck out." I shrugged. Shit, it wasn't like she didn't know what was up. If that ain't what she was here for, then I had no use for her.

I needed to shower anyway. I had a party that I was trying to step through tonight, and a trip to the mall was needed, so I didn't have time for her bullshit. I wasn't a flashy nigga by a long shot, but I did like nice shit, and shoes were my guilty pleasure. I headed to the back of my apartment and prepared to get myself together.

"So you just gon' leave me sitting here?" Quinia pouted from the living room where I left her dumb ass.

"Yep."

Nothing else needed to be said. I shut the bathroom door and let the sound of the shower fill my ears. I didn't have time for her dumb ass. Shit, as far as I was concerned, if she wasn't sucking my dick or bent over in front of me, I didn't have shit to say to her. I'd just find me a new broad to slide up in tonight.

I undressed and hopped in the shower and let the water beat

down on my back. I had to get the thought of Lala in those tight ass pants out of my head. It was getting harder and harder to keep this platonic. My body deceived me more often than not, and the thought of her with someone else bothered me more than I would like.

Lala was beautiful, and she knew it. She was half black and half Cuban with skin the color of toasted almonds and hair down her back. Damn what I wouldn't do to wrap that shit around my hands and beat her pussy up from the back. I knew that pussy was good because she was stingy with it. She wasn't a virgin, but she didn't sleep around. I knew that for a fact; I made it my business to.

I heard the bathroom door open and shut and rolled my eyes in the back of my head. I wasn't with her shit today.

Quinia has lived in the Creek for as long as I can remember. When she got old enough to live on her own, she moved out of her mom's and got her own apartment. Quinia played the system to the max; food stamps, utility checks—you name it, she got it. She loved how she lived and had no ambitions of changing anything about her lifestyle. That was one of the many reasons that I didn't want nothing more from her than a quick nut.

"The fuck you want, Quinia? I got shit to do." She didn't respond, so I figured she'd turned around and left back out, until the shower curtain opened, and there she stood ass naked.

My eyes traveled over her body, and I had to admit, she was bad as hell. Quinia was what you would call a red bone. She was short as hell with wide hips and an ass to match. Her round face and chinky eyes made her look Chinese, but her thick pouty lips let you know she was definitely black. She was beautiful none-theless, but that's all there was to her.

Stepping into the shower, she instantly dropped to the floor and took me into her mouth. I watched as she bobbed her head on my semi-hard dick, until he stretched to his full potential.

"Fuck!" I gritted.

Her eyes immediately met mine, and I watched as the corners of her mouth turned up into a smile with my dick still in her mouth. I hated a cocky bitch, so I grabbed the back of her head and began to fuck her mouth deep and hard. She tried to keep up, but I was blessed below the waist, and the way I was moving caused her to gag and not in a good way, but I didn't stop; I kept fucking her mouth until I released down her throat.

I pulled out and looked down at her, and she had tears in her eyes. I couldn't feel sorry for her. She allowed herself to be treated like that, so I was not about to take responsibility for her feelings.

"So that's it?" she asked and then looked at me, still on her knees.

"Yeah, I'm good." I shrugged.

"Well damn, can I at least have a few dollars since you got to nut and I didn't?"

She wondered why I treated her like I did? Here was a prime example. I pointed to the outside of the shower. She went to say something, and I gave her a look that said don't fuck with me right now. She smacked her lips, wiped her eyes, and got out of the shower.

I stepped under the water and tried to release the aggravation that I was currently feeling. Once the water started to get cold, I stepped out of the shower and wrapped a towel around my waist. Entering my room, Quinia was sitting at the head of my bed on one of my pillows where I lay my head. She knew I hated that shit, I wasn't trying to sleep where her ass had been. I walked over and pushed her ignorant ass on the floor.

"What the fuck you do that for?"

"You know I don't play that shit." I glared at her. "I don't know where yo' ass been."

"I bet if it was your precious Laurence, you wouldn't say shit. That bitch can do no wrong." She rolled her eyes.

"You got damn right, because I know she ain't out here slanging pussy like she getting paid for it." I dropped my towel and walked to the mirror that was attached to my dresser. I looked through the mirror and watched her watching me with a scowl on her face.

"That bitch ain't all that." She scoffed.

"She's more than you are." I chuckled.

"I don't know why I deal with you," she said under her breath, thinking I wouldn't hear her, but I did.

"Get the fuck out then. I ain't begging you to be here." I held my hand out toward the door, and she stared at me with her chinky ass eyes. When she was mad, she looked like she had smoked a pound of weed to the head. "Why the fuck you still sitting here?"

"Whatever, Heart. You gon' give me some money or not? I need a fit for the party tonight." The only reason she was trying to roll through was because she knew I would be there.

I walked over to my dresser and peeled off two one hundred-dollar bills and threw them at her feet. I turned and walked to my closet to pick some shit out to head to the mall. I had to meet up with Mitch and Lake before I turned up for the night too, and I was already running behind.

"Really? Why do you treat me like this?"

"Why not?" I popped my head out and shrugged then disappeared into the closet again.

I opted for a pair of stonewashed Levis and a red Ralph Lauren polo with my black and red 11's. I put lotion on my arms, dabbed on some cologne, and grabbed my phone and keys. "You can go," I said without even looking at Quinia as I walked to the front of my apartment.

She huffed and mumbled something from my room as she finally walked up to the living room, and the defeated look on her face was hilarious to me, so I laughed.

"What's funny, Heart?"

"You."

"One day you gon' realize my worth."

"I damn sure hope you realize it first."

Speechless, she walked out of the apartment with a scowl on her face. When she slammed the door, I couldn't help but laugh. I didn't know what to tell her; it was what it was and wasn't shit changing. There were only two choices in the matter: accept it or get the fuck on.

Grabbing my phone and shooting La a text, I grabbed my keys and headed out the door to scoop Lake so we could hit North Lake before it got too late.

LALA

*S*tate Employees Credit Union was always crowded on Fridays. Shit was ridiculous. I waited in line for a good twenty minutes. All I needed to do was to make a deposit. There was a guy up there holding up the line arguing with the teller about her putting money in the wrong account. The teller was telling him that it was a simple fix, but he just wanted to argue. I wanted to cuss him out for her and for holding up the line. When he finally turned around to leave, I realized that it was Mitch. I tried to turn my head so that he didn't see me, but it was too late.

"Hey there, beautiful." He smiled once he saw me.

Mitch supplied all the drug dealers in the Mooresville area. He was something like a hood legend around the way. He took over a year after my dad was gunned down, and he was still pushing. Heart worked for him, so I was familiar, even though Heart made it his business to keep me away from him.

Mitch was a sexy man. His tall six-foot-three frame, chocolate skin, and lips that were made for pleasing a woman, had my hormones raging. I had to bite my lip to bring myself out of my lustrous thoughts. Not only was this man paid, he was ten years my senior and out of my league. Plus, my heart was with Heart.

"What's up, Mitch!" I giggled like a little school girl. If Heart even saw that I was talking to Mitch, he would have a fit. He always said that Mitch was no good for anybody but himself. Mitch was a very dangerous married man, and Heart said it was best to steer clear.

"I'm good, beautiful; better now that I've seen you." His smile was infectious, so I couldn't help the one that spread across my face. "That award winning smile of yours makes my heart jump every time I see it." He moved the piece of hair that fell across my face and placed it behind my ear, letting his hand linger a little longer than it should. "Will I see you later?"

"Next in line, please," the teller said, letting me know that it was my turn.

"Um I—I ha—have to go," I stammered.

He chuckled. "I'll take that as a yes."

"Next in line, please." I turned to look at the teller, and she tilted her head as if to tell me to hurry up or she was gon' take the next person. I rolled my eyes and turned back to Mitch.

"I have to go." I turned to walk to the teller, and he grabbed my arm and handed me a wad of money. I surveyed the money, and it had to be at least three grand. "Um, I can't take this," I whispered.

"Well if you can't, I will. Hell, just like if you don't take yo' ass on, you gon' be shit out of luck. People got shit to do while you sitting up here cupcaking with this fine ass man," the older lady that was behind me said. I looked at her and smiled. She better be glad I was respectful to my elders.

"You're gonna get me cussed out." If Heart found out I took money from Mitch, he would have a fucking fit, and I would never hear the end of it. To keep the peace, I tried to give him back the money, but he shoved it back in my direction.

"Don't insult me. Take it. No strings attached." He winked, and it was something sneaky about the way he did it, but I just took it and went to the teller before I lost my spot. I decided not to put all of it in the bank. I put the four grand that Heart gave me and one out of the wad that Mitch gave me.

Once that was done, I called Duke Energy and paid the light bill and reconnect fee. I called and paid the rest of our bills while I was in the parking lot. After all the bills were paid, I took a deep breath and leaned my head against the seat. My phone rang, and I looked down and saw that it was Miracle, my bestie.

"What up doe?" she said before I could even greet her.

"Shit, what's good?"

"We sliding through DLo's party?"

"You already know."

Miracle was my girl. She was the first person that I met when I had to move to the Creek. I didn't know anybody because I went to a private school, and my dad wouldn't let me anywhere near the hood, so all of it was new to me when we had to move. My girl Miracle welcomed me with opened arms though, and I would forever be grateful. She and Heart made the transition that much easier.

"Bitch, what you wearing?" she asked, popping on her gum.

Her twentieth birthday was right around the corner, so she was celebrating all month. Her age did not match her body. Miracle was a full-blooded Cuban, but she was born in the U.S., so her accent wasn't as thick as her sister's and mother's. Her shape made porn stars hate her. She was around five feet six with wide ass hips and a round ass that looked like you could detach it and use it as a shelf. Her breasts were perfect double D's and sat up real nice. That's the one thing I didn't have, so I always gave her hell about hers. Her exotic features made her the interest of every dude in the hood, except Heart, and the envy of every bitch. My boo was a baddie.

"'Bout to hit the mall in a few."

"What you pushing? Hell, it don't even matter; come scoop me."

"I got the Impala." I grinned because I was the only person that Heart let drive his cars. Miracle started clapping her hands.

"You may as well go ahead and fuck him and get it over with. Claim that dick and live happily ever after." She was so outspoken and was my and Heart's biggest fan.

"Shut the hell up, Miracle; that's my best friend," I whined, because I knew that deep down if I was given the opportunity to be with him, I would, no questions asked. "I'm on my way, heffa." I hung up on her because I didn't want to hear her speech about how stupid I was for agreeing to this friendship thing.

I couldn't deny my feelings for Heart, and it was getting harder and harder to hide them. I wanted that man. I understood where he was coming from when I was younger, but now I was grown as hell. I didn't get why he still shied away from the thought of us being more than what we were. I knew he loved me —his actions showed me that—but his mind wouldn't let his heart speak, and it was starting to piss me off.

I really didn't know how much longer I would be able to deal. Every man I came in contact with, I compared to Heart, and the minute I did, the chance of them being anything in my life was canceled, and it sucked.

❧

"*Y*asssss, girl, you betta." Miracle cheered me on as I modeled this short black romper that cupped my ass just right, with some thigh high boots. This was a house party, and I didn't know about wearing heels because things could get crazy, but I was just that cute that I considered sacrificing.

"I love this store." I beamed as I turned around to see how the outfit hugged my curves. We were in Charlotte Russe at Northlake; you could get bomb ass clothes for cheap as hell.

I had money, thanks to Heart and Mitch, but that didn't mean I wanted to spend it all at one time. I had to teach myself to be better with money. It was hard as hell to go from an unlimited supply of money when my dad was living to having to struggle because my moms lost her damn mind. I was learning though, which is why Charlotte Russe was my favorite store.

"Me too. I think I'm getting this." Miracle held up a small ass pair of leather shorts and a lace crop top that looked two sizes too small.

"You trying that shit on?"

"No. I don't need to. I'll make it work," she said, and I looked at her like she had lost her mind. "What?" She shrugged and we both laughed.

We looked around a little more to make sure that we got what we wanted. I walked up to the register and ran smack into Quinia and her dumb ass sister Lanae. I tried to walk around her so I could pay for my shit, but she blocked my path every time I tried to get around her. I had to take a deep breath because I knew I was in nursing school and wouldn't be able to get a job with an assault on my record, and I heard Heart's voice in my head... *"She ain't got shit to lose—you do."*

I looked down and tried once more to get around her, and this time she let me. I looked to the sky to thank the man above because I was two seconds from knocking her the fuck out and dealing with the consequences later.

"The word is excuse me," she said, and her sister laughed. I turned my attention to Lanae.

"Damn, I thought you had kids, so why in the hell you out here acting like one." I glared at her, and she stepped up like she was gon' do something, but Quinia stopped her.

"I wish you would." Miracle came from across the store so

fast I barely saw her. "She got shit to lose, I don't! I'll fuck you up," she warned, and they both took a step back.

Miracle was in cosmetology school and was almost done. She had dreams of opening her own salon, and until then, she was gonna work for a local stylist in our area and pay booth rent, so she didn't have to answer to anyone.

"Fuck her, Lanae. Let me spend my man's money." She pulled out two measly one hundred-dollar bills, causing me to laugh. I pulled out what I had left from the wad of money that Mitch gave me and started counting off twenties so I could pay for my things.

"Your man blessed us both I see." I looked over, and her face was red as hell. You could see the hate that she had for me pouring through her eyes. That wasn't even the money that Heart gave me, but she didn't know that. "Miracle, come on. Outfits on Heart tonight." Miracle and I both laughed. After I paid for our stuff, I looked at Miracle. "Let's go cruise the city in the Chevy. Heart left me a tank full of gas."

I knew I was being petty, and I probably should have just left the situation alone, but she stayed trying to start shit with me, and it was my turn.

"Girl, if you don't yank that bitch bald, I will," I heard Lanae tell Quinia.

"She knows better; all it takes is one phone call," I said over my shoulder.

She could talk all she wanted, but she knew like I did that she wasn't about to put her hands on me and live to tell about it. I could handle my own, but with Heart, I didn't have to. Turning the corner, I ran right into Lake. I looked up at him, and he had a smirk on his face, but he wasn't looking at me. I snapped my fingers in the air to get his attention. "Where's Heart?"

"I'm right here." I felt his arm wrap around my shoulder before I heard his voice. He leaned down and kissed my cheek.

"You gon' make ya girlfriend in there blow a gasket." I giggled and looked up at him. He leaned down and kissed my lips and looked over at Quinia and threw her a head nod. I shook my head, turned in her direction, and shrugged my shoulders. She rolled her eyes and pretended like she was shopping and wasn't just fucking with me.

"Petty ass." Heart chuckled and pulled me into a hug. "You handle that?"

"Now you know I did." He nodded his head and grabbed my bag. He peeked inside and then started looking through it. He held up the romper and gave me a look that said I knew better. When he got to the boots, he lost it.

"Fuck no! Take that shit back right now!" He was loud as hell; even turned the heads of a few patrons that were passing by.

"No, Heart. I'm trying to find me a man tonight," I joked, but he didn't see shit funny, he grabbed my jaws and squeezed them tight.

"Don't get fucked up." He growled lowly in my ear and shocked the hell out of me, so much so that I froze in place. He was pissed, and for once, I was on the receiving end of it. My eyes met his, and for a minute, I tried to I explore his thoughts, looking for some kind of indication of what he was feeling at this moment.

This was the first time that I had seen Heart like this. He wasn't the jealous type when it came to me; he just would always tell me to be careful. Right now, he was acting like I was more than his best friend. I guess he shocked himself too, because he got this weird ass look on his face, handed me my bag back, backed away, and took off in the opposite direction. Watching him walk away without another word left me confused to say the least.

"Aight, y'all. Be safe, and don't be drinking and driving," Lake said, pointing to me. "I'll see y'all later." He winked, but again, it wasn't to me. I looked over at Miracle, and she was cheesing like a Cheshire cat. I had to snap a few times to get her attention.

"What the fuck are you doing, Miracle?" I glared at her.

"What? Girl, nothing. Let's go. I'm hungry, and we need to get to the liquor store before Mr. Jones get off. You know he the only one that be hooking us up." I hit her with the side eye.

I warned Miracle about Lake a long time ago when she came to me about being interested in him. Lake had a family with my girl Mira who was like a big sister to me. So Lake stepping out on Mira for Miracle, left me in a bad place, because I loved them both. Miracle knew how I felt about it, and I prayed she respected it.

"I ain't playing with you. You know he with Mira, and she good peoples."

"She aight." She frowned, and I shook my head. "She don't like me though." She snickered.

"'Cause of that." I pointed from her to where Lake just stood.

25

"He's never gonna leave her, so don't play yourself." I grilled her.

"How about you worry about you and Heart." Her demeanor became defensive, and I wasn't feeling it. I wasn't trying to get into with my girl, so I took a deep breath to calm myself.

"Out of respect for me." I touched my chest.

We stared at each other what seemed like forever. So many thoughts were going through my head. I was starting to think that there was something that I didn't know until she smiled.

"Girl, I told you I ain't on that. I wouldn't do that to you." I nodded my head, letting her know that I heard her, but something was telling me that she wasn't telling the truth. I didn't have any proof, so I left it alone for now.

"That grown ass man don't want yo' ass anyway. He just be playing with you," Lanae said coming out of Charlotte Russe with Quinia in tow.

"Ohhh, you think he want you? What, to play stepdaddy to yo' snot nose ass chaps though?" Miracle put her hand under her chin like she was thinking. "Hoe, go play in traffic." She waved her off and looked at her nails like she was bored.

"That's what's wrong with you little bitches. Somebody needs to whoop yo' ass one good time. I bet you learn then." Lanae was only five years older than me and acted younger.

"You wanna be my teacher?" Miracle stepped toward her. Quinia looked down at her phone and then up at me. She grabbed her sister and shook her head.

"Nah, chill, Nae. Let's just go," she said in a defeated tone.

"That nigga tell you what to do, not me. Fuck him."

"Girl, let's go. I got the money, and if you don't bring yo' ass, you won't eat." Quinia rolled her eyes and struck out in the direction of the food court.

I shook my head because she was sitting here running her damn mouth about shit that didn't have anything to do with her, and she didn't even have money to feed herself.

She stood there for a minute with her arms folded tightly across her chest. I would never understand why she thought that her opinion of anything that was going on with me and Heart mattered in the least. As much as I should ignore them, I must say that they got under my skin at times, but I would never let them see me sweat.

"You better go if you want to eat; you look hungry," I said and pointed in the direction of Quinia who was long gone. She flipped me off and stomped off in search of her sister. Me and Miracle burst out laughing.

"Let's go eat so we can get ready to stunt on these hoes tonight," Miracle said, dancing in the middle of the mall where we were still standing.

"Bet." We high fived and headed to eat and hit the liquor store before our connect got off. I was ready to turn up and have some fun. I needed it.

QUINIA

$\mathcal{H}$ate is such a strong word, but it doesn't begin to describe what I felt for Lala. I didn't know what it is about her that made Heart fall all over her, but he did, and I despised it. She was perfect in his eyes; she could do no wrong, but to me, she was just a half breed hood rat.

I'd done everything possible to get Heart to look at me like he looked at her. Whenever he needed me, however he needed me, I was there with bells on. He still treated me like I was nothing when it came to her. I wished she'd die.

"Why the fuck you let her talk to you like that!" Lanae yelled on me, and I rolled my eyes because she would never understand. When I said I would do anything to get Heart, I meant that, even if it meant looking stupid in front of that bitch.

"Just let it go, Lanae, damn."

"No, you just stupid, and don't ever talk to me like that

around them again." Ahhh, that was what she was really mad about because I told them bitches she was broke. "Got them thinking my pockets dry and shit."

"Bitch, they are. What you mean?"

My sister was a leech. Whenever she could put herself in a position to come up or latch on to someone who was, she was there. Right now, me fucking with Heart was benefitting her, which was why she was so passionate about me correcting Lala and taking my place as his girl.

What she didn't know was that I tried so hard to do just that, but Heart just wasn't taking the bait. He was gonna be my way out the hood if I could get him past Lala. Heart was the man that everyone wanted; he was sexy, and he was hood rich. He may not have had the huge house and the hundred thousand-dollar cars, but he could do for me what no other man in my sights could.

"Fuck you. The only reason you got money is because Heart laced you up." She waved me off and then chuckled. "From the looks of it, Heart giving yo' ass chump change compared to what ol' girl was spending." She laughed, and I pushed her on her ass.

"You think that shit funny? Well get yo' own fucking food." She jumped up and pushed me.

"Bitch, you find yo' own way home then." She walked off, and I thought about it. Mooresville was a long way from Charlotte. I caught up with her and apologized. We stopped at Wendy's, grabbed something to eat, and then headed over to her baby daddy's crib.

She had kids by the local wannabe named Jason. He was the

most backward hustler I knew. He did coke and smoked more weed than he sold. He was always taking money from Lanae to re-up, which is why she was always broke. I couldn't count the number of times he blew her income tax checks, and she was still chasing after him.

I couldn't really say anything or give her any advice, because I was the same with Heart. Only difference was, he was the one giving me money and not the other way around. Heart just didn't give a damn about me, and Jason actually cared about Lanae; well, at least I thought he did.

The way we were with men was disheartening at times, but it was the way we grew up. Our mother never showed us what to expect from a man because she had a new man every time you turned around. She used them for what she could get, and when they were out of money or merely tired of taking care of her, they bounced, and she went back on the prowl for her next victim.

She taught us at a young age to use the system as much as we could. "Ain't nothing like free money," was her motto, and we lived by those words. For as long as I could remember, my mom had never worked. She always had a man to take care of anything she needed.

"I hope Lil' Jay ass ain't here," I said, getting out of the car when we pulled up to another set of projects called Sedgefield that was across town from the Creek.

"Girl, you shouldn't have fucked him like that." Lanae laughed.

I made the horrible mistake of getting drunk and fucking Jason's cousin one night. He told me he had come up on a lick and was about to be making some money. I quickly found out that he robbed somebody, and that's how he got the money that was gone in a few days. He was back to being broke, and that definitely wasn't my type.

He was persistent in seeing me after the first night I fucked with him, but I wasn't with that. I didn't deal with broke. I'd rather Heart treat me like shit every day but lace me than deal with a man that I had to take care of.

"Girl, don't remind me." That was one of the worst nights of my life that he made sure to remind me of every time I saw him.

Lanae walked up to the door and knocked; that was another thing that bothered me. Why did they live in separate apartments across town from each other and they were together with kids? I never understood that. What was even worse was she didn't have a key to his place.

"What's up, babe," Jason said the minute he opened the door. He was putting off this nervous energy, and the fact that he kept looking back and forth between the door and Lanae let me know that there was something or someone in there that he didn't want her to see. "What you doing here?"

"What you mean what I'm doing here?" She tried to get in the house, but he wouldn't let her in. "Move, man."

"Why didn't you call?" He flashed a nervous smile and tried to reach back and shut the door, but my sister pushed past him, and he stumbled into the house.

"Why didn't I call? When have I ever had to call? What the hell is wrong with—" Her words trailed off as she looked into the eyes of the mystery woman that sat comfortably on the sofa like she belonged there.

"Jason, who's this?" she asked, tearing her eyes away from the TV that had her attention before the festivities began.

"Yeah, Jason, who in the fuck is this," my sister said sarcastically. Although she tried to be hard, I could hear the pain in her voice, and it pissed me off.

"Listen, Lanae, let me holla at you in the back."

"Nah, you can holla at me right here. What kind of games you playing, Jason. I'm home taking care of your kids while you doing God knows what with—" She waved her hands in the air. "—Her."

"Ohhhh, you're the baby mama?" She smiled toward Lanae. Either this chick was confident in her position in his life or she was just that clueless. "I can't wait to meet the kids."

"Meet the—" my sister started but finished her sentence with her fist that connected with the mystery chick's mouth. She repeatedly hit her until she drew blood. All that could be heard through the tiny apartment was Lanae's licks and ol' girl's screams for help.

"Cut this shit out, Lanae!" Jason yelled, pulling my sister off the girl. As he was pulling her up, she tried to kick Lanae, and that's where I stepped in. "Lil' Jay! Nigga, come help me, shit!" I heard Jason call out. All of a sudden, I was lifted and carried to the back of the apartment. I was kicking and wiggling, trying to get out of his hold.

"Chill, Quinia," he said against my back. He was struggling to restrain me. "Damn, girl. It's me, Lil' Jay." He released me, and I was about to flip the fuck out and go off on his ass, but something on the bed caught my attention.

"What's all that?" I pointed to the money on the bed and all the stereo systems that were lining the wall of his room. He must have been robbing people again. One day he was gon' hit the right person, and they were gonna hurt him, but for now, I was about to help him spend this money.

"I been making moves." He smiled like he was rolling in the dough. He was nowhere near where he needed to be to bag me, but I'd hang for a minute. "I got a few more moves to make tonight, and I'll be straight for a little minute."

"Well, I gotta go deal with my sister and your dumb ass cousin's shit, so make sure you hit me up tomorrow and we can chill." I kissed him on the cheek and eyed the money again.

"Aight, babe. I got you." He licked his lips and grabbed a few bills. "Here... take this and buy you something nice." He winked.

Shit, he handed me $300, more than what Heart gave me. *I might just have to give him some, but not now*. I had to get to DLo's party because I knew Heart was going, and I'd bet my life that Lala's bitch ass was gonna be in attendance. I had to run major interference. I was not about to let her have what I was trying to make mine permanently.

I talked to Lil' Jay for a while and then went back upfront to find my sister, who was arguing with Jason by the front door. I looked around for the other chick, but she was nowhere to be found. Once they got their shit together and she forgave him, we were on our way. I had to get to that party.

HEART

I didn't know what just came over me, but I didn't like that shit. Seeing that outfit and those boots had my dick hard just picturing her in it. Hearing her say she was wearing it for someone other than me, had me on one, and I didn't know how to handle it. I needed to get my shit together because I knew that I wasn't what she needed right now, but my heart was ignoring that, and my emotions were taking over my actions.

Lala needed to finish school and become something great. Me and my lifestyle would prevent her from that. The way I lived my life could interfere with the way she was trying to live hers, and I couldn't have that. Even though most people knew how I felt about La, I made sure that none of my decisions affected her. If we were together, there wouldn't be a way to separate the two, at least that's how I saw it in my eyes. So as bad as I wanted her, I was gonna do what was best for her, and that was not being with her the way we both wanted.

"Yo, what was that shit about?" Lake asked with a fucked-up grin on his face.

We were en route to see what our boss Mitch wanted with us. We already knew that there was a shipment coming in, and he needed help breaking it down, and as payment, he was gon' lower his prices for us for this pickup, but that wasn't for another three days. A few of his guys got pinched, so he was short staffed. We didn't mind helping; we did that shit all the time, so what he wanted was a mystery, and I wasn't feeling it.

"Mind yo' got damn business. Wanna be all in my shit. What the fuck you doing with Miracle's wild ass?" I glanced at him and then turned my attention back toward the road. "Mira gon' fuck you up." I chuckled.

"Mira ain't gon' do shit but sit at home and do what she do best—take care of my kids," he said, texting away on his phone with a huge smile plastered on his face.

"Keep on and another muthafucka gon' be playing stepdaddy to yo' kids." It was my turn to smirk. The way his face contorted at the thought of someone else giving his girl what he failed to give her was amusing.

"And that will be the day that they both meet their final resting place." He grilled me, then he returned to his signature smirk. "Just like Lala gon' find her another nigga to give her that act right."

I looked over at him and shook my head. I was not about to let him know that what he just said pissed me off. The show I put on at the mall was enough, so I just chuckled and turned up the radio. As far as I was concerned, the conversation was over.

"I thought so," he said over the music. All I could do was shake my head.

Lala owned my heart, and if I could give her everything she deserved, I would, but right now, it wasn't in the cards for us; at least that's what I was telling myself.

Our whole vibe was different today though. When I kissed her it felt different; I couldn't describe it, but it was. I know that La had been with other men before; although I didn't like it, I didn't have a choice in the matter. When she said something about finding a man, I didn't understand why I got so upset.

"What the fuck this meeting about?" Lake reached over and turned down the radio. He sparked one of the blunts that I had rolled stashed in the ashtray.

"Fuck if I know. He already talked to us about breaking down that shipment, so I don't know what the fuck he wants."

"Bet," he said and then turned the music back up. I reached and grabbed a new blunt and lit it up and took it to the face. My attention was drawn to the lake as we pushed it back up 77N.

I remember when Big L first died, and Lala and her moms moved to the Creek. She would just sit on the stoop and cry. I would go over and sit with her and tell her about how good of a dude Big L was to all of us in the hood. She was amazed that I knew her dad. He never let his family venture out into the hood. As far as they were concerned, this place didn't exist.

To get away from the madness of her reality, I would take her out to Lake Norman and just sit and talk. It was then that I realized that she was wise way beyond her years and that she was special. Almost made me want to be a different person for her, but my reality wouldn't let that happen. I was who I was and that was that.

"Who the fuck is all these muthafuckas?" I asked when we pulled up.

"Shit if I know."

Hopping out of the Tahoe, we headed up the long ass driveway leading to Mitch's crib. He lived in a nice ass house that was off Highway 3 going toward Kannapolis. It wasn't an over the top house. Considering how much money that nigga had, I would say the house was modest at the most.

There were niggas everywhere when we walked in; muthafuckas were stressed than a muthafucka. I wasn't feeling that and was about to jet, when Mitch walked in like he was a fucking Don or something.

"Welcome." Nobody said anything; everyone just stood and looked at him, waiting on him to tell us what the fuck he wanted. "So you know we had that little raid in Statesville the other day?" Again, no one said anything. "A little birdie told me I had 5-0 in my camp, but that can't be true, can it?"

That shit caught my attention. I started looking around the room, trying to see who was gon' show their cards and immediately knew who the fuck it was. Menk was squirming in his seat, making sure to look down and not make eye contact with anyone in the room.

I was low key pissed off because that nigga had come down to the Creek on more than one occasion to hang out and chill.

Hell, he had dropped off some work for us a time or two, so did that mean I was on the police radar? Reason went straight out the window; my gun came out of my back, and it was at his head in a matter of seconds.

"Whoa, Heart!" Mitch said with his hands out and a smirk on his face. "You seen that shit too, huh." He chuckled, and so did his right-hand, Mello.

"This nigga drops work off to the spot... He chilled with me and the crew. The fuck," I said through gritted teeth.

"I got you," Mitch said with his hands still out. I grinded my teeth and looked at Mitch without moving my gun from the back of Menk's head. "Chill. He 'bout to help himself out."

"Nah, fuck that." I took the safety off and then I felt a piece of steel on the back of my head that made me laugh.

"The man said chill," dude barked.

"You think that shit mean something to me." No sooner than I got that out of my mouth, all I heard was *crack* and then a body hit the floor. I looked back, and the dude that had the gun to my head was on the ground leaking, and Lake was standing over him with his gun to his head.

"Muthafucka, you done lost yo' mind," Lake growled. *My nigga.*

I turned my attention back to Mitch who had a frown on his face. I shrugged my shoulders, and he laughed. "Let me take care of this shit." His tone was calm, but his demeanor was demanding. "There is more to it, and he's the only muthafucka that can tell us that." He raised his voice a few more octaves.

I lowered my gun and turned to look at Lake and nodded. He

backed away from that big ass black muthafucka that was on the ground, but not before he kicked the shit out of him. We both walked back to the door and stood directly in front of it in case somebody tried to make a move.

"Cocky muthafuckas," Mello said under his breath but loud enough for us to hear him. I looked at him and smirked.

"What all do they know, Menk?" Mitch asked, pacing in front of the couch that Menk was sitting on.

"I don't know what you're talking about, Mitch," he cried out.

"I'll ask you one more time, and then you gon' piss me the fuck off." He glared at him, but Menk didn't say anything. "Maybe you need a little motivation." He nodded for Mello to turn the TV on, and when it came on, you could see a woman and two small kids bound and blindfolded. Mitch picked up his phone and made a call. "Tell your husband to tell me what I wanna know before y'all pay for his mistakes."

"No, Mitch. Don't do this, man. Please, they're innocent. They ain't got shit to do with this," he cried. "Baby, I'm so sorry."

"Just tell them, Menk, please." His wife sobbed, followed by wails from his kids.

"Aight, aight. Just let them go." He stood up, and Mitch rocked his ass, and he fell right back on the couch.

"Nah, tell me what the fuck I wanna know, then I let them go."

"Detective Ringo ran up on me during a drop and arrested me. He told me that if I helped them catch you that they would let me go. They don't want no one but you. They don't give a fuck about us. They said you killed a cop, and they want your head." He sniffled. "I couldn't go to jail and leave my family."

"What do they know?"

"They know what I know." He finally looked in Mitch's direction, and if looks could kill, he would have been a dead ass. "I'm sorry, Mitch, but my family..."

"I've always told you that if you ever get into trouble, let me handle it. Why didn't you listen to me, Menk? At the most, you would have had to stay overnight. I got people in place for shit like that. Which is how I found out about you." He smirked, and Menk really started to sob. This little cat and mouse bullshit was starting to get on my nerves. "Now your family will never see you again." He gave Mello the cue to turn the TV off. The guy that Lake cracked over the head and another guy carried a screaming and pleading Menk downstairs to what I guess was a basement. "Y'all are dismissed. This is what happens when you cross me."

I chuckled and turned to walk out of the door. There wasn't a man alive that put fear in my heart. The way I looked at it was, if it was my time, it was my time, and I was gon' take that shit with my head held high. You was gon' have one hell of a fight trying to take me out though.

"What the fuck was that shit?" Lake laughed as we climbed in the Tahoe. We didn't even wait to see if that nigga had anything else to say. "Who the fuck is he supposed to be, The Don or some shit? Fucking clown." We both laughed.

"I should have pulled the fucking trigger is what I should've done." I'm not good with authority. I hated a muthafucka that tried to tell me what to do; a nigga wasn't built like that.

"Fuck all that. I need a drink and a blunt after that bullshit," Lake said as I pulled out and headed straight for the ABC store.

I grabbed a blunt and lit that bitch up, and Lake followed suit. I chiefed all the way to the liquor store. I parked and finished off the rest of my blunt, ashed it, then looked toward the door to see how crowded it was, and my eyes met Lala's. This was not what I needed right now. Her young ass shouldn't have been in the fucking liquor store anyway.

We piled out of the car, and my eyes followed her to my Impala that I didn't even notice sitting there. She opened the door and looked back at me. My lips had a mind of their own because they spread into this goofy ass smile, and she smirked and got in the car. When she rode by, she made sure to make eye contact.

"What the fuck, man." I adjusted my dick in my pants.

I was jolted from my thoughts by Lake laughing. I looked at him and flipped his dumb ass off. I hated his bitch ass. I grabbed a bottle of Crown Vanilla, and this nigga grabbed some Cîroc. We were about to be turnt like a muthafucka. I just hoped I could keep my shit together.

~

"*B*odak Yellow" was blaring through the speakers in DLo's crib, and the bitches were going crazy. I don't know what the hell it was about that song; whenever females heard that shit, they went nuts. I admit it went hard though.

"It's packed than a muthafucka in this bitch!" Lake yelled over the music. "Fuck! Mira calling. Let me go see what she wants. Lil' man had a fever earlier; I need to make sure shit is okay."

"Nigga, take yo' ass home and check on yo' seed," I scolded.

"Mind yo' got damn business and worry about all the niggas staring Lala down."

He pointed in the direction of the front door that she had just come through. It was like time stopped as she took one step at a time, perfectly in rhythm to the song that was playing in my head. The way that little ass jumper shit she had on clung to her body had me ready to go through this bitch handing out fades like it was my fucking job. Damn that girl was beautiful.

She was headed in my direction until Quinia jumped in my lap. I tried to move her, but I was sitting on a stool, and the way she did it had my legs stuck behind her body weight. By the time I had her off me, Lala was nowhere in sight.

"Damn. I thought that was just your best friend." I ignored her and subtly scanned the room for Lala. "So why yo' dick hard? I been in yo' face all night and this ain't happened." She grabbed my shit, and that got my attention.

"Because my dick bored as fuck." I snarled my nose. She was about to piss me the fuck off, and the bad thing was I didn't even know why. We had been chilling since I got here, but the minute Lala walked in, my mood changed the fuck up. Shit was getting crazy.

"Aye, why you looking all mean and shit," Lala said, ignoring Quinia sitting here beside me. I smiled because I knew she would come and find me. I grabbed her by the back of her bare neck because she had her hair up in a bun. I hated when she did that shit. I pulled her to me and kissed her lips like I normally did. Quinia inched her way back in my lap, but my attention was still on Lala, and she pretended like she wasn't even there.

"You know I hate that shit," I said reaching my hand up in her hair and untwisting the bun she had up there.

"Come on, Heart. You know how long my fucking hair is, and it took forever to get that bun right," she whined.

"You shouldn't have even done the shit."

"I didn't know if I was gone have to smack a bitch." She smirked.

"You know good and damn well ain't nobody fucking with you." I glanced down at Quinia, who was sitting there watching the exchange between the two of us. I snatched the ponytail holder out of her hair, and her beautiful hair fell down her back. "Beautiful," I said out loud, not meaning too.

Her eyes darted in my direction and then out into the crowd, and my eyes followed hers to see Miracle walking in our direction.

"Bitch, you know how long it took me to get all that damn hair in that bun?" she fussed.

"Blame him." Lala pointed at me and snaked her neck.

"Ohhhh, daddy said he like to run his fingers through them long tresses." She giggled, and Lala gasped and hit her in the arm.

"Man, what the fuck! You act like I ain't sitting here," Quinia fussed like someone gave a fuck.

"Get the fuck on then," I said in an even tone. When she didn't move, I looked down and said, "That's what the fuck I thought."

Yo Gotti's "Rake It Up" came blaring through the speakers, and Miracle grabbed Lala by the arm and dragged her to the makeshift dance floor in the living room. Them two singlehandedly shut shit down. They had the attention of everybody in attendance; even the women looked on in envy. My eyes were glued to the way Lala was working her hips and ass. My eyes caught hers a few times, and she smirked and shook her ass harder.

Quinia sat in my lap and watched me watch Lala and shook her head the entire time like I gave a fuck. I didn't know what I was feeling right now, but I needed to get it under control because it wasn't right. I didn't deserve her. I wasn't good for her. I knew that if I showed interest, she would feed off it, and we would end up in a position that wasn't good for her.

Lala's eyes met mine once more, and I smiled at her and raised my eyebrow which caused her to giggle and shrug her shoulders. She was showing out, and I knew it was for me.

"I mean, y'all are pretty much eye fucking." Quinia rolled her eyes and crossed her arms across her chest.

"You mad? You can always get the hell on."

She didn't move, just like I thought. She just sighed and relaxed into my arms. I chuckled at how dumb bitches could be. I continued to watch the little show that Lala was putting on for me. It wasn't until I saw Mitch walk up behind her that I was over her little dance routine.

He stood behind her and let her bounce her ass on him, and a nigga was tight. I didn't even realize how mad I had gotten until I heard Quinia scream from me throwing her on the ground. I stood up and was about to make my way over there until Lala saw me watching and started in my direction. I tried not to give a fuck about what she did, but the one thing I was against was her being with Mitch.

That nigga was married, and his wife was sneaky and scandalous as fuck. If she found out about him fucking around with Lala, she would be on that bullshit. I knew if she did something to hurt Lala, I would have to kill her, and that meant starting a war with Mitch. I would if I had to, but if I could prevent it, I would. Plus, that nigga wasn't shit; he fucked for sport. Lala would be just another notch under his belt, and she was better than that.

"Hey, you okay?" she asked, walking over and standing in front of me. I grabbed her and pulled her in for a hug while looking directly at Mitch who had a smug look on his face.

"I told you about that nigga," I said into her ear. I felt Quinia's hand on my back, and I shrugged her off and threw over my shoulder, "You doing too much." She rolled her eyes as I focused my attention on Lala. "Stay the fuck away from him, Lala."

"Okay, Heart, chill," she said, putting her hand on my chest, and I immediately calmed down.

"What's good, Heart." Mitch walked up and dapped me up,

and I nodded my head at him. "Is this what you spent the money I gave you on?" Mitch bit his lip as he looked Lala up and down.

"You taking money from this nigga, Lala?" That shit burned me up. I wanted to cuss him and her out, but I kept it chill for the moment.

"It wasn't like that, Heart. He didn't give me a choice. He put it in my hand and wouldn't take it back. I told him I was straight," she explained.

I didn't care what the fuck was coming out of her mouth. She shouldn't have taken shit from that nigga, especially since I had just given her money. I let her go and sat back on the stool. Quinia's ass found her way back in my lap, and I let her. The look that Lala gave was mixed with a bunch of different emotions.

I didn't know why I was so fucking mad. We were just friends, but the thought that she was taking money from him and he would possibly be getting something out of it, pissed me off. Lala wasn't that type of girl, but I knew how niggas like Mitch operated. He had a talk game on him, and he would sell her a dream she wouldn't be able to wake up from.

"Shit, I thought y'all were just friends. I was gon' ask lil' mama out, but if she's spoken for..." Mitch threw his hands up in mock surrender and chuckled. Lala looked at me, waiting on my response.

"She grown as fuck and can do what the fuck she wants to!" came out of my mouth before I had the chance to stop it. I didn't mean that shit. I wanted her to stay the fuck away from him, but it seemed as though she knew what the fuck she was doing; she was taking money from the nigga.

"Oh yeah?" Lala asked. I didn't know what the fuck was going on with us as of lately, but the look in her eyes was something that I had never seen before. "Sure. I would love to go out with you, Mitch." She turned her back to me and faced him.

I bit down on my back teeth. I wanted to yolk her ass up and lay his ass out, but I had to keep my cool. I didn't want to step in because she would think that it meant something that I didn't want it to. Just then, Lake walked up with Miracle who looked on with confusion written all on her face.

"Cool. Let me get ya number, and I'll call you and we can hook up soon."

She called off her number, and they made plans to talk later. He said his goodbyes and then left the party. Lala gave me a hateful look, and then she grabbed Miracle's arm and stomped out the door. I wanted to go after her, but I didn't... I couldn't, but we would be having a conversation about this shit.

MIRACLE

"**I** can't believe he did that." I listened as Lala cried about how Heart played her in front of Mitch and that bitch Quinia. I didn't know why she tried to play that they were just best friends thing; everybody knew better. They might not have had sex, but they wanted too, and there was more there than just friendship.

"Girl, you should have told that nigga that." She was talking a lot of shit now that we were gone. For as long as I could remember, Lala had never been one to bite her tongue, so it was crazy to me why she was so tight lipped when it came to Heart.

"It ain't that serious." I twisted up my lips and gave her the side eye. "It's not." She looked at me and then turned her attention back to the road.

"I'm starving. Let's stop by Waffle House since yo' ass broke up all the damn fun and shit. Got niggas fighting over you and shit." I rolled my eyes playfully, and she giggled.

"I didn't have them fighting over me. I don't know why that fool Mitch even said anything about the money he gave me. It wasn't like I asked for it." She pouted. "I don't want to go out with him."

"So why in the hell did you agree to it?"

"'Cause Heart played me."

"I thought he was just your best friend?"

"He is!"

"So what does it matter? I'm confused. You mad because he didn't tell you not to go out with this nigga, and he mad because you taking money from that nigga? Y'all both just need to stop playing and shit and get together, then you wouldn't have to worry about this."

"Miracle, it ain't that easy."

I had been knowing Lala since she moved to the projects after her dad died. She was cool as fuck. Most people didn't fuck with her because of who she was, but I didn't give a fuck about all of that. She was cool, and we clicked. We had been tight ever since, and I couldn't imagine her not being in my life.

We could tell each other anything, which is why I didn't understand why she was trying to tell me that she wasn't in love with her best friend. Hell, I couldn't talk. I was keeping something from her too.

"Easy for what, you to admit that you love that man?"

"What!"

"Oh, you heard me. I've been watching y'all do this little

song and dance since you were fourteen." I giggled. "I'm not the only one that sees it—everyone does. It's just there. It's not something that you can just fake. What y'all got is real, and it's up to y'all to make it work."

She didn't say anything. I could see her nibbling on the corner of her bottom lip. Sighing deeply, she took the back of her hand and wiped the tears that had left her eyes.

"I love him, Miracle. I always have, and my biggest fear is that he doesn't feel the same way I do. I know he loves me as a friend, but I could really see myself with him."

"You don't have to tell me that. I already know this."

She glanced over and smiled. Whipping into the Waffle House, there was a group of women chilling in the parking lot. When they saw the car, they flocked to it, hoping that it was Heart. Me and Lala giggled. When we opened the door and they saw it was us, they were so disappointed.

"Sorry to disappoint, ladies." Lala waved as she strutted across the parking lot with me close behind.

"Why you always in his car?" the one girl asked right as we were about to enter the restaurant.

"Why the fuck you worried about it? He ain't yo' nigga, and even if he was, I'm always gon' be here." Lala was more defensive than she had ever been. Normally, I would jump in and add my two cents, but tonight my girl was on one, so I let her handle it. "All you bitches are just the same, chasing after a man that you will never be able to call your own. I own the blueprint to his heart. Just keep playing yourself."

"Well," I said as Lala walked in and headed straight to the

bathroom. I knew that she was crying. She hated for people to see her cry, but she always cried when she was mad. I followed her and knocked on the door that I realized was locked.

"I just need a minute, Miracle."

I backed away and headed to an open booth. I was looking over the menu when I heard the bell chime, and Lake walked through the door. I damn near salivated. That man was something sexy. His light skin housed some of the most interesting tattoos that were perfectly placed. His smile was perfect and brought attention to his handsome face. He wasn't super tall but at least six feet, and his athletic build was a turn on in itself.

He looked around the restaurant in search of Lala because he knew that we left together. "What's up with yo' sexy ass," he said, sliding into the booth that I was in.

"I'm hoping you soon." I bit my lip.

"You know I got you." He smiled as he grabbed for my hand, but I heard the bell ring again. Heart walked in with that bitch Quinia. I shook my head. "It ain't like that. That bitch followed us here. She's like a fucking leech."

Heart walked right up to the table. "Where she at?" he asked through gritted teeth, and I pointed to the bathroom. He headed in that direction with his little puppet right behind him. I wanted to laugh, but it was kinda sad she was that desperate. "Yo, stop fucking following me the fuck around, shit!" Heart barked, and even I jumped at how harsh his words came out. But in true bird fashion, she sucked her teeth and came to the table where me and Lake were sitting.

"Nah, you can't sit with us. I don't fuck with you." She

looked to Lake like he was gon' say something other than what I said. I wish the fuck he would have. "Don't look at him. You better take yo' ass on somewhere before you piss me off. Again, I ain't got shit to lose."

She smacked her lips and sat in the chairs along the wall that was designated for people with to go orders. I laughed at how stupid she was making herself look. What Lala said to those other girls was very true; no one would ever be what she was to Heart, no matter how much they tried or followed him around.

"Open the fucking door, Lala, before I knock it the fuck down." Heart's voice boomed throughout the restaurant. Every person's eyes in the establishment went toward where he was standing, but he didn't care. He was on a mission to get into that bathroom. I guess Lala took his threat to heart, because the door came open, and she tried to push past him, but he looked at her face. "The fuck you crying for, Lala?" When she didn't say anything, he pushed her ass right back in the bathroom.

"Them two just need to stop fronting and fuck, damn," Lake said, shaking his head, causing me to laugh and Heart's puppy to smack her lips. "Yo, you know all you are is pussy to him, right?" Lake asked, and Quinia ignored him. "Well sit yo' dumb ass over there and look stupid then. You know like I know that he don't give a fuck about you."

The waitress came over, and I ordered both me and Lala the All-Star Breakfast to go. I had a feeling after that conversation in the bathroom, she was gon' be ready to leave. I was completely okay with that because the sooner I got home, the sooner Lake could come through.

"I can't wait to bend that ass over," Lake said, rubbing my leg under the table.

"Shit, I can't wait for you to." I tucked my lip in between my teeth and squeezed my legs together to keep him from moving up any further. I shook my head at his sexy ass.

Lala was completely against me fucking with Lake, but I couldn't help it. By the time she warned me, I was already head over heels in love with him. Yeah, I knew he had a girl, but he didn't love her. He wanted to be with me, but he needed to get his situation together first because he had kids. I knew that sounded like game, but he meant it. He proved to me that he did.

I hated to lie to Lala, but he made me promise to not tell her because she was friends with his girl, and he said that she wouldn't understand. He was right, because the minute that Lala thought that I was feeling Lake, she told me to stay away from him. Lala was my girl, but I was grown, and the heart wanted what the heart wanted; she should understand that more than anyone.

Us being together was only half the secret, and if anyone knew the shit we shared, it would be a lot of mad muthafuckas. I'd proven my loyalty to him, and I was just waiting for him to do the same.

"I remember the first time I saw ya little young ass." He looked up to the sky like he was picturing the moment he saw me at the park chilling with Lala.

I was fifteen. It was right when Lala moved down. Heart was coming to visit Lala and give her money. When they walked off to talk, I was left there with Lake. We flirted and talked about school and stuff. He told me that if I was a little older, he would show me everything that I had been asking for.

The day that I turned eighteen, he became my first sexual experience, and we'd been rocking ever since. I couldn't help but to fall for him; it was hard not to. He was sexy as hell, and his presence in the bedroom was out of this world.

"Love at first sight," I said and looked at him to see what his response was gonna be. I had been telling this man I loved him for as long as I could remember. "You know that *forever* type of love."

"You wild," was all he said before all hell broke loose, and our attention was diverted to the bathrooms where Lala and Heart were.

"Just leave me alone, Heart!" Lala yelled before she stormed out of the restaurant.

"Nah, fuck that!" Heart yelled after her before he turned to Lake. "Aye, take my truck and Miracle home." He was out the door before any of us could say anything about what he just demanded.

"What the fuck!" Quinia yelled and then ran after them.

"Bitch, give it up!" I screamed to her back, and she flipped me off. "I hate that bitch." I shook my head.

Lake paid my bill, and we walked out and got into Heart's Tahoe. Right as we were about to get in the car, a Mercedes came wheeling up fast as hell. I looked at Lake, and he put his head down and looked at me.

"Yo, get in the car and don't say shit unless I fucking tell you," he said in a hushed but forceful tone.

"Who is that, Lake?" I asked, completely ignoring what he had just said.

"Do what the hell I said, Miracle," he said a little louder.

I slid in the soft leather seats and focused on the car that came to a quick halt right in front of Heart's Tahoe. Out jumped this beautiful woman. She had a honey complexion that was flawless. Her beautiful gray eyes lit up in the night. Her body was sick and had me staring at her like she was about to be my next meal. I was so mesmerized that it took me a minute to realize that it wasn't Mira, so who the fuck was she, and why was she here? I cracked the window in the truck so I could hear what they were saying.

"What the fuck is going on!" she yelled with her hands on her perfectly sculpted hips. "I'm already competing with your girlfriend. I'll be damned if I'm about to compete with some young bitch."

I had to let what she just said sink in. So this was not his girl? This was another bitch he was fucking outside of me and her? What the fuck kind of shit was he on? I opened the door and climbed right on out and joined the festivities. Lake had some explaining to do.

"What happened?" I asked and stepped to the front of the car. "Lake?"

"I told you to stay in the fucking car!" he said through gritted teeth. His eyes were telling me to back off, but the way my heart was set up, I wasn't about to do that. I knew about Mira, but according to him, I was the only other woman in his life. I saved myself for this man, and the way I saw it, he belonged to me when he wasn't with Mira and his kids. "Miracle, go get in the car."

"Nah, I'm trying to figure out who she is. She ain't Mira, so there's no conversation to be had." I tilted my head at him.

"Who I am is none of your concern, little girl. Go do your homework or something." She popped her gum in true ghetto fashion.

"Shut the hell up, Wynn. Miracle, just get back in the car. I'm gonna get you home right after I finish this." He gave me a caring look as if I was just someone he was helping out.

"So this how we doing shit?" I crossed my arms across my chest. He gave me a warning look, and I nodded my head. I took off toward the Denny's that was across the street, pulled out my phone, and copped an Uber. Fuck Lake!

LALA

I didn't know why I was so mad about all of this. Somewhere deep in my heart, I wanted him to fight for me in that moment, and the fact that he just pretty much handed me over to Mitch hurt me to my heart. I was pissed, and there was nothing that he could say to make it better.

"So you ain't gon' say shit, La?" I sighed because all he could talk about was the fact that I took money from Mitch. I kept telling his stubborn ass that it wasn't like that, but he didn't believe me. "I know you hear me fucking talking, La."

"Got damn it, Heart, it wasn't like that. I don't know how else to say it." I threw my hands up. "He saw me at the bank, he put the money in my hands, I told his ass no, and he walked away. End of fucking story." I turned to face the window, signaling that the conversation was over. He was pissing me off, and I wasn't for it.

"So why did you tell him that you were gonna go out with him, Lala?"

"Why did you tell him that I could?"

"You know what the fuck I told you about him!" He yelled so loud that it caused me to jump. He had never talked to me like that before, so I was taken aback by it. The rest of the ride home, I didn't say anything, I could feel him looking at me every now and then, but I focused my attention out of the window.

As soon as the car stopped, I jumped out and ran all the way to my apartment and shut and locked the door. I went to the window to see if he followed me or not, and he hadn't. He was standing outside looking up at my apartment while that bitch Quinia stood behind him with her hands on her hips.

"The fuck wrong with you, little girl?" my mother slurred. I smelled her before I saw her coming down the hallway. I wasn't in the mood for her shit. I just wanted to go to sleep. Heart had fucked up my night, and I didn't want to deal with anyone. I just wanted to forget. "I know you hear me talking to you."

I pushed past her, and she grabbed my hair and pulled me back. I snatched away and balled my fist. I wanted to lay her ass out, but I refrained. I counted backwards from ten and kept it moving.

"You ain't too old to get your ass whooped." She pushed me, and I tripped down the hall. I was trying to keep my composure, but she had one more time to put her hands on me, and I was gonna forget that she was my mother.

"And you ain't too drunk to get yours whooped either, Cynt." I pointed at her.

"Ya fast ass walking around here with ya ass on ya shoulders. I ain't one of ya little friends." She turned around and headed for the living room.

"Alcoholic bitch," I thought I said under my breath, but evidently, she heard it, because the glass that she was drinking out of came whirling down the hall and landed in the back of my head and shattered, that's how hard she threw it.

All I saw was red. Reason went out the window, and I completely forgot that she was my mother. Pissed was an understatement. I headed straight down the hallway and punched her dead in the face. I could tell that she was shocked because I had never put my hands on her, but tonight, she crossed a few lines.

I had to have blacked out, because when I came to, I was being pulled off her, and she was screaming "help" to the top of her lungs. My eyes went to her face, and she was all bloody, and for once, I didn't give a fuck about her and her wellbeing. Once I calmed down, I would probably feel bad for putting my hands on her, but right now, I felt like she deserved it.

"Let me go." I struggled against the person that was carrying me out of the house.

"Chill the fuck out, Lala." It was Heart. He squeezed me tighter until I calmed down. Once he had me calm, I broke down in his arms, and he held me. Something was different. "It's gonna be okay, Lala."

Normally, I believed him when he told me that everything was gonna be okay, but after tonight, I didn't want to hear anything he said. I jerked away from him, and he looked at me like I was crazy. I couldn't explain what I was feeling right now, because I didn't know. I felt like Heart kinda threw me away tonight, and I couldn't deal with that right now.

Backing away from him, I could see the confusion on his face, but he didn't stop me. He just stood there with his hands in his pocket, watching me. A part of me wanted to run and jump in his arms, but I knew that it would just be on a friend tip, and that was starting to not be enough. To keep from hurting myself, I turned and ran.

I ran until I reached Ms. Marsha's house. She was the property manager who lived in the house directly across from the Creek. She was always close with my daddy, and if I knew any better, I would have said that they were having an affair, but my dad really loved my mom. She had a daughter that was in middle school, and she helped us out tremendously when my dad died.

"Who's banging on my door like that!" she yelled on the other side. She must have looked out of the peephole, because I heard her squeal then the door flung open. "Child, what happened to you?"

She touched my head and pulled back her hand and it was full of blood. I didn't even know that I was bleeding. As she ushered me in the house, I stumbled a bit. I was starting to feel lightheaded.

After cleaning me up, she made me a pallet on her couch and helped me lay down. This is what I missed about my mom. When I was hurt and I needed her, she was there. I didn't know who the hell that monster was that just attacked me. It didn't take me long to doze off.

I was awakened by the smell of bacon and coffee in the air. I stretched out and tried to open my eyes. The light coming through the window caused a sharp pain to shoot through my eyes, and it was then that I remembered the fiasco from last night.

"You ready to talk?" Ms. Marsha asked, not bothering to look at me. Her focus was on the food she was cooking. "Who did this to you."

"Cynt." I was finally able to sit up and focus my eyes.

"Drunk?"

"Yes!" She shook her head and started fixing plates. "Where's Michelle?" I asked about her daughter.

"She's gone with my mother, yard selling." She chuckled. There was an awkward silence. "Heart came by here this morning."

I wanted to smile, but I knew that me and Heart would have to have a serious conversation about everything that happened last night. My only fear was that it was going to change everything about us. I couldn't worry about that though. I needed to be looking for somewhere to stay because I couldn't go back there.

"Did I have my phone with me? I need to ask Miracle if I can stay with her for a little while until I get somethings in order. I can't go back there right now."

"You are right about one thing—you can't go back there. Your mom is sick, and she needs help. Right now, you do everything for her, and she's tearing you down in the process. I've never seen you like I did last night." She shook her head. "I've got two apartments open, but I will only offer you the one at the top, in the corner."

She looked out of the top of her glasses. She always did that when she dared you to argue with her. I didn't want to stay at the bottom anyway. That's where everything I was trying to get away from was. I needed to get away from that.

The top and the bottom of the Creek was like day and night. You wouldn't even think you were in the same complex if you didn't know any better. The bottom of the Creek was where all the action was: the drugs, the fights, and the drama. The top was where the families lived. It was nice and quiet, just what I needed.

"I'm good with that. I need to focus on school anyway."

"Well, my dear, you didn't have a choice," she said, and we both laughed. I had to grab my head because it was banging. I couldn't believe my mom hit me with a glass.

After we ate, we talked about everything that I would have to take care of in order to move in. She went down, and we did all the paperwork, and she gave me my keys. Thank goodness I still had all the money that Heart and Mitch gave me. With that, I would be able to furnish my new apartment along with the little paycheck that I would get from Walmart in a few days.

"Thank you so much. I don't know what I can ever do to repay you." I hugged Ms. Marsha.

"Girl, you better get on somewhere. Lawrence would haunt me in my sleep if I ever let you go without. You can always come to me, know that." I nodded my head. She had always been someone that I looked up to, but I never wanted to burden her with my issues, so I never laid them on her.

We talked a little more, and then she left me with my

thoughts. I sat in the middle of the floor in my new apartment. I was finally on my own. Somewhere in the back of my mind, I couldn't help but to wonder how my mother would make it without me, but I couldn't let that hold me back anymore. I had to worry about me, especially seeing as though she didn't.

I ran through my head everything that I would have to do to get my apartment ready. Marsha was giving me thirty days to switch the lights, but I would be doing that Monday right after class. She had done enough for me.

I was gonna call Mira up to see if she would take me furniture shopping, I didn't need much, and I would settle for a nice bedroom set and living room set from Big Lots. I needed to be smart with the money that I had left. I didn't plan on asking Heart for anything else. I didn't know what I was gonna do about school next semester, but I would figure it out. However, I was about to stop asking him for shit starting now.

"Are you okay?" Mira asked the minute she answered the phone.

I loved Mira; she was like a big sister to me. She had enough on her plate, so I didn't go to her with my problems, but she always seemed to know what was going on with me before I did.

"Yeah, why you ask?" I tried to play it off.

"Don't make me smack you, heffa," she threatened, and I smiled. "I already heard about that shit ya mama pulled. I almost came down there and beat her ass again. If you need somewhere to stay, we have two extra rooms in the basement, so you'll have complete privacy."

"I got my own apartment. That's what I was calling you for, to see if you would take me furniture shopping."

"Wait, what? It's Saturday. How the hell you pull that off?"

"Ms. Marsha looked out for me. I went to her house last night after all that shit went down."

"Why didn't you call me? You knew I would have come and got you."

"I didn't want to bother you, Mira, and it looks like I went to the right place anyway. Ms. Marsha hooked me up."

"Sounds like it. Well my mom has the kids, and Lake didn't bother to come home, so give me an hour, and I'll come and get you," she said just like I knew she would.

Mira had the sweetest heart, and it killed me to know that Lake wasn't being one hundred with her. I didn't have proof, because he refused to do anything in front of me because he knew how tight we were, and I was thankful for that, but I knew he wasn't what Mira thought he was.

"K. I'm at the top now, second building on the left. Apartment 3B."

"Okay, lil' mama. See you in a few."

We hung up, and I laid back on the floor and stared up at the ceiling. Heart immediately rushed to my mind. I knew that our friendship was changing. I just hoped that we could figure it out before it was too late. On my end, I needed to stop depending on him for so much, and that was all there was to it. We had been so close for so long, it was gonna be hard, but it needed to be done.

LAKE

*W*ynn fucked a nigga shit all up last night. Miracle was pissed as hell and wouldn't even hit a nigga back. I had feelings for her little ass, and I couldn't deny that shit, but I loved Mira, and I didn't think there was a woman alive that could ever come in between that. She had my heart, and that was that.

Wynn was a fucking mistake that I wished I had never come in contact with. She was what you would call the forbidden fruit. She was married, and if her husband ever found out, it would cause a lot of problems for me. Once again, my dick got me into some shit that I couldn't get out of.

"So who was the little trick last night," Wynn said, coming out of the bathroom. We were held up in a little apartment she got for when she wanted to spend time with me. As hard as I tried to dodge her, Wynn wasn't exactly the kind of woman you said no to. She was sneaky as shit and would get what she wanted by any means necessary, which was one of the reasons why I was still fucking her to this day.

"What I do when I ain't with you is none of your business. The way I see it, you getting this dick is the only thing you should be worried about. Yo' ass gotta whole husband."

"And you got a wife."

"She ain't my wife, but that ain't yo' business either."

"Look, the way I see it," she said mocking me. "I got you by the balls. Now you can leave the little tramp alone, or I can tell my husband what the fuck we been up to, and we both know how that goes." She stuck her pointy ass nail in her mouth. I was getting tired of her fucking threats.

"Go ahead. Shit, what if I tell him for you?" I raised a brow, and she laughed. "You think shit funny? I'm almost over this shit."

"Okay, look, Lake. Let's not do this. I just wanna make you feel good. Don't you want me to make you feel good?" Before I could answer, she had my mans down her throat and lightly sucking.

"Oooh, fuck." I can't lie; this was the other reason I kept coming around. Her head game was fire, and she was down to try just about anything in the bedroom. "Suck that shit just like that." I grabbed the back of her head and guided her head to my liking.

Once she brought me to my peak, she sucked down everything that I released, making sure she didn't leave a drop. I just laid there looking at the ceiling just thinking about how the hell I got myself into this bullshit and how I was gone get the fuck out before it caught up with me.

Luckily, right before she was about to mount me with no condom on, her phone rang, and it was her husband, and she had to go. I wondered where in the hell she told him she was all night, but I guess that wasn't my business.

"I'll call you later." She smiled.

"Nah, I'm spending time with my woman for the next few weeks. My black ass been doing too much, and I ain't trying to fuck up my home. Nah mean?"

"No, I don't know what you mean. You know how this works."

"I don't know shit. I don't know who the fuck you think I am, but you need to pipe that shit the fuck down." I raised up slightly. She didn't say anything. She just glared at me before she slammed the door and left me there in this fucked up ass silence.

I hated the quiet because it gave me too much time to think, and I didn't want to think about this shit I had going on. I didn't know what the fuck I had got myself into. I could see this ending one of two ways, and I wasn't prepared to deal with either one of them. If Heart found out about this shit, he was gon' flip the fuck out. I had to figure out a way to end this shit and fast before it blew up in my face.

Jumping up and hitting the shower, I walked to the closet full of clothes and shoes that she had purchased for me, selected my fit for today, and got dressed. I grabbed my favorite cologne Acqua Di Gio by Giorgio Armani and dabbed it on then hit the door, being sure to lock it.

I hopped in my Chevy Camaro and looked on the seat, and there was a wad of money just lying there. It had to have come from Wynn. I shook my head, scooped it up, and slid it in my pocket. She was always doing shit like that, and it kept my ass coming back, just like her little bitch. I had money, but a nigga was greedy. That shit was gonna be my downfall.

Pulling out of the apartment complex, I rolled onto the street and watched as Mira went rolling by. I tried to duck, but she saw me and hit the brakes. I had to think of a quick ass lie because I was in different clothes than the ones that I had on when I left the house yesterday, and I smelled fresh. I couldn't tell her that I was out working all night, because my appearance didn't match that.

"Who the fuck lives here, Lake." Mira jumped out of the car, leaving it on, and in the middle of the street. I slowly slid out of my car like my ass wasn't guilty of anything. "When I talked to you last night, you said that you were gonna be out of town until this morning, but here you are." I had forgot I told her that bull-shit. Fuck!

"Yo, you can't leave the car there!" I yelled out, trying to stall.

"Fuck that shit, Lake. Where the fuck you coming from?"

"I just did a drop off. Now get in your car and get the fuck away from here before you start some shit, and it won't be good for either of us," I said through clenched teeth to make it real.

She searched my face to see if I was lying or not. I could tell that she didn't believe me, but just in case, she walked backward to her car, never taking her eyes off of me. Opening the car door, she slowly slid in and pulled off. I pulled out my phone and tried to call her, but she cleared me, and after the third call, she blocked me. I was gon' get in her ass about that shit because I told her ass I didn't play that shit.

I took off toward the Creek so I could talk to Heart about the reup and possibly check on Miracle if she wasn't at school or on that bullshit. When I got to the entrance of the Creek, I noticed Mira pulling into the first section, so I pulled in right behind her. She didn't know anybody down this bitch but Lala, and Lala didn't live at the top, so what the fuck was she doing here? I whipped in right behind her and blocked her in so she couldn't pull out, in case she was fucking around or some shit.

"What the fuck you doing down here, Mira?" I yelled, walking up to the driver door and yanking it open. "Who the fuck you know in the fucking Creek?" I was hot as a mutha-fucka. I didn't know if it was guilt or if I was scared that she would actually move on from me. I knew the shit I did wasn't right, but I wasn't about to sit around and see her do the same thing.

"Muthafucka!" She got out and slapped the hell out of me, and I grabbed her by the neck and threw her against the car out of reflex. She started to swing on me. I knew I had fucked up royally when I heard Lala behind me, hitting me in the back telling me to let her go. I let her go, and she swung and punched me in the mouth, and I grabbed my shit and glared at her. "I ain't the one running around here lying and shit! I'm sick of you and your disappearing acts." Her chest heaved up and down. "I've never gave you a reason to think I was up to shit, but you on the other hand." She bit her lip and shook her head. I reached out to touch her, and she slapped my hand down. "I'm tired, Lake. I'm tired."

"Mira, take my keys and go up to my apartment." Lala handed her, her keys, and I looked at her all crazy. "Yeah, I got my own shit, and Mira was here to help me get furniture." She rolled her eyes.

"No, fuck him. Come on. We got shit to do." Mira hopped in the car and slammed the door. Lala looked at me and shook her head before she joined her. Mira rolled the window down. "Move that piece of shit before I move it for you." She didn't even look at me, but I could see the tears streaming down her face. I was fucking up.

"Let me talk to you, baby. I'm sorry. I don't know what the fuck wrong with me." I tried to reach in the car, but she put the car in reverse and rammed her Ford Expedition into my car. "What the fuck!" I had to jump back before she hit me.

"Move the fucking car before I hit it again," she cried out. Her beautiful round face was drenched with tears... had a nigga hating himself.

I tried to put my hand in her window again to pull out the keys, but she rolled it up and pulled forward and reversed again and again until she was able to get around it. I looked on as she pulled out of the parking lot. My fucking car was fucked up. I would have to take the money that Wynn gave me to get that shit fixed.

"What the fuck going on, nigga? Ms. Marsha called me talking about I need to come get you 'cause you putting yo' hands on a woman." Heart had a mug on his face as he walked up in mine.

"Chill, nigga. Mira down here tripping." I couldn't tell him the whole truth, 'cause that would make me have to say where I was last night. "I saw her up here, and I didn't know who the fuck she knew up this bitch, so I pulled up." I shrugged. "Wasn't nobody but Lala, but the damage was already done."

"You putting yo' hands on Mira, nigga?"

"Nah, her little ass hit me, and I grabbed her up. You know I wasn't putting my hands on her." Heart looked at me and then at my fucking car, causing me to shake my head.

"She did that shit?"

"Hell yeah. I was trying to talk to her ass about how I reacted, and she went the fuck off. She told me to move or she was gon' move it." I dropped my head. "She's a woman of her word." I had to laugh to keep from getting more pissed than I was. Heart joined in.

"That's what the fuck you get, nigga. I told yo' ass."

"Fuck you, nigga. What's up with this shipment?"

"Shit, we gotta go pick that shit up in a few."

"Aight, bet. Follow me to drop my shit off at the fucking shop so I can get it fixed." He laughed and said that he would be ready in a few. A nigga needed to get his shit together and fast before I lost my woman amongst other things.

MIRA

J didn't know what happened to me and Lake's relationship. We used to be so good together, but lately, he had been on some other shit. Staying out late if he even came home, lying, and now the nigga had the nerve to put his hands on me. I had half the mind to stab him in his sleep. We never used to treat each other like this. We were the Bonnie and Clyde of the hood, until we moved out of the hood. After that, it was like a switch went off, and Lake went crazy.

We had twins, a boy and a girl, Larken and Laken, who had just turned five years old. My main focus was being a mother, so I wasn't in the business of chasing his ass around. I expected for him to be there for his family, and financially he was. As of late, that was all he did. I was tired of hearing all the 'you know what I do' excuses, because it was bullshit, and he knew it. All darkness came to light though.

"You okay, girl?" Lala asked from the passenger seat. I loved her like she was my little sister. She was so sweet and caring. I just felt like she was dealt a bad hand, but she was making the best of it, and I respected her for that.

"Yeah, I'm just over Lake and his bullshit. I don't know what has gotten into him lately, but he's been doing some dumb ass shit, and I ain't with it."

"Yeah. I've never seen him act like that before. He was like a completely different person."

"If you know he was fucking around, you would tell me, right?" I glanced at her out of the corner of my eye. Lala and I had bonded over the years. I knew how her mother was. She needed someone to be on her side, and I made sure that I was there. I just hoped that the loyalty was reciprocated.

"Girl, you already know, and if I see it, I'm stepping in right then and there. I don't play that." She snarled up her nose, and I high fived her. "You ain't even got to ask that." I nodded my head.

"Was he with y'all last night?" I remembered him telling me that he had to go out of town last night but would be back this morning.

"Yeah, we went to this house party off of Patterson. DLo threw it," she said carefree, not knowing she had just blew up his lie. "Heart pissed me off and I left. I went to the Waffle House, and they showed up a little while later. Me and Heart got into it and left, and he stayed." She shrugged.

"Well I caught him coming out of Stone Creek Apartments this morning. Who the fuck he know out there? Only reason I saw him was because I had to go and take Larken's inhaler to my mom before I came to you."

"I don't know anybody way out there, but we can go scope that shit out if you want. You know I'm down to ride." She threw her hands out.

"Nah, that shit gon' come to light. But if I change my mind, I'll let you know."

We went into Big Lots to see what they had as far as furniture so that she could furnish her new apartment. I didn't even know that Big Lots had furniture like this. She ended up getting a nice ass couch and table for her living room and a bed with a dresser for her bedroom and a desk for her spare room, all for under two grand. The sales guy was a little sweet on her and even offered to deliver it for her.

We went to Walmart and Dollar General so she could get the essentials for her first apartment. She said she didn't want to get anything from her mother's but her clothes. Back at the apartment, we put up everything that we got from the stores. She got a text that the guy from Big Lots was on his way. After all that was done, we went to get her clothes, and thank goodness her mother wasn't home.

Once we got everything put up and set up, it was after midnight. I made sure she was straight and headed home. I was tired, and Mama was keeping the kids again tonight, so I was about to go home, hit that shower, and relax with a glass of wine.

I was dreaming that Lake was kissing on my inner thigh. It was feeling so good that I didn't want to wake up, so I tried my hardest to keep my eyes closed. It wasn't until I heard his voice that I realized that it wasn't a dream.

"I'm sorry for the bullshit, baby. I'ma do better. I put that on my life." My eyes met his, and my heart both fluttered and ached at the same time. Something was telling me that the "bullshit" that he was speaking of had more to do with his absence lately and what he did earlier today. "I love you, Mira, and no matter what, that will never change."

I didn't say anything; I just let the warm tears that were pooling in my eyelids pour out onto my face. I was so tired of crying over this man. There was a time in our relationship that he would do everything in his power to see me smile. Now it was like his hobby was to hurt me. I didn't think he fully understood the extent of his actions. If he kept this shit up, he would definitely find out.

My body began to respond to him, even though I didn't want it to. I struggled against his touch, but the minute I felt his warm tongue grace my clit, I released the flood gates. His thick tongue slowly assaulted my secret place, and I couldn't help the moan that escaped my lips.

"Spread them pussy lips so I can do what I do," he said in between licks.

I did as I was told, and he rewarded me with his award-winning head game. The way he sucked, licked, and lightly nibbled on my button had me running from the tongue. He got me when he licked from my slit to my clit, over and over again.

"Yesss, oh yesss." As hard as I tried to keep my moans to myself, I just couldn't help it any longer. I gave the man all that he was working for. "I'm about to cum!" I squealed.

He latched on to my clit and alternated from sucking to licking until I exploded into his mouth. All that could be heard throughout the room was my heavy breathing and the sound of my wetness as he continued to roll his tongue through it.

"Damn I missed this," he said between licks.

"Umm, well maybe you should come home more," I said, and he stopped licking and began to kiss up my thighs.

I had to bite my lip because he was stirring up feelings in me that I hadn't felt in a while. Don't get me wrong, sex with Lake was always good, but the romance and intimacy was lacking. It was always like we were fucking lately—no love was there. But tonight, it was different. I had the old Lake back, even if it was only because he messed up.

He made sure to show just as much love to both thighs before he continued his journey up to my stomach, but not before he French kissed my kitty one more time. Once he reached my stomach, he took a dip into my belly button and lingered for just a second, causing my clit to throb.

"I will always know where home is," he said between kisses. "A nigga been fucking up, but I promise you I got my priorities straight now. Don't give up on me." He continued his journey until he reached his destination.

Staring into my eyes, he told me that he was sorry without

saying a word, and I believed him. My only problem was I didn't know exactly what he was sorry for. Right now, I was gonna relish the moment and pray that whatever he had done, it wouldn't break us.

Taking his knee and spreading my legs, he lowered himself so that his dick was at my opening. His lips crashed against mine right as he entered me slowly.

"Ahhhhh," I released as he rested on my g-spot and slowly began to beat it. "Oh my goodness. Shit, I miss this," I cried out right before his lips met mine again.

He worked his hips to the beat of my panting until he brought us both to a needed orgasm. We were both breathing heavy and could barely catch our breaths. I hadn't cum like that in so long, and I needed that.

"I love you, Mira."

"Don't hurt me, Lake," was my response. I hoped like hell we got ourselves together and quick, because I loved this man, and I wanted to be with him for the rest of my life. I just wasn't about to be a fool to do it.

HEART

I hadn't really talked to Lala in about two months now. She was doing everything in her power to avoid me, and she was pissing me off. All that was about to change today though. I was poppin' up at her job the minute she clocked in. She had class today, and I knew that because I went to pay her tuition for next semester and asked the financial advisor for her schedule. After agreeing to take her out, which would never happen, she gave it to me. I started to pop up there, but I knew she needed to concentrate.

"Hey, baby." Quinia walked over to the green box that I was occupying at the moment. I was hoping that she could see the aggravation on my face, but no such luck.

"The fuck I tell you about that baby shit?" I took a pull on my blunt that was dangling from my lip.

"Dang, I was just saying hey, Heart." Her hands found their

way to her hips, and her neck did a little dance to the rhythm of her attitude. "Anyway, what we getting into today?"

"I don't know what the fuck you getting into, but I can promise you that it doesn't involve me." Ever since that night of the party, I hadn't been fucking with Quinia like that except when I wanted to get my dick wet. She was taking the little attention that I did give her to the head, and I needed to get a grip on that. She felt entitled, and I wasn't with that shit.

"Humph. Lala must be up your ass again. You been walking around here like you lost your best friend, and now you talking to me like I ain't shit to you."

I finished my blunt and dropped the roach on the ground and stepped on it. I looked at her for a minute and took in her appearance. Her round face and chinky eyes made her look innocent, but the whole damn city of Mooresville knew that was a lie. If Quinia wasn't so got damn aggravating, she would make some man a damn good girl, but that man would never be me. Whether I wanted to believe it or not, my heart was taken.

I elected not to answer her, so instead, I turned my attention to Lil' Jay, a nigga that owed me money. When he saw me standing there talking to Quinia, he took off running, and that pissed me off because a nigga hated to run. He hit the back of the building and took the path through the woods that led you to the street behind the Creek. *Wrong move!*

As soon as I caught up to him, I pulled out my gat. *Pow!* I let off a shot that whizzed by his head. He fell to his knees, trying to dodge the bullet. "Move, muthafucka, and take ya last breath." I walked up to him with my gun trained on him. "Got my ass out here running, knowing I got asthma." I grabbed my chest.

"I got ya money, man. I was just on my way to pay you."

"So that's why you ran?" My gun met the side of his face. "First you steal my shit out of my car, and I let it ride." I hit him again. "You sold my shit, and I let that shit ride because of who you are." I hit his ass again. "All I asked was for my money for my radio, and you dodging me?" I hit his ass again for good measure.

I went in his pockets, and that nigga had about a thousand dollars. I took all that shit. He didn't owe me but like five hundred for my radio, but that wasn't the point. He stole from me, and I let him live, then his bitch ass stiffed me for the money. I had to set an example because if I let this shit slide, every muthafucka around here would try me, and I would have to show them why it wasn't a good idea; I didn't have time for that shit.

Beating Jay's ass was already causing an issue that I didn't want. He was Mitch's fucked up nephew, and I was sure I would hear about this, but he couldn't say much seeing as though he didn't fuck with him like that either.

"Aye, man. I only owed you five," he said through bloody lips.

"Bitch, this is interest." I threw his wallet at his head. "Next time, I swear you won't walk away. Stay the fuck away from me."

I made my way back to the green box, pissed as fuck that that nigga made my ass run and catch him. I pulled out a cigar and my sac to roll up; had a nigga stressed and shit. Just as I finished rolling up, Lake pulled up at the same time Quinia walked back up. I rolled my eyes in the back of my head and sighed heavily.

"Got damn! You like a fucking leech. Get yo' ass on some-where," Lake said, snarling his nose up at Quinia. "He don't want yo' ass. I don't know how many fucking times he can show you. Got damn." I handed him the blunt and laughed at his dumb ass.

"Fuck you, Lake. You always got something to say."

"What's up, nigga?" I dapped him up and pretended that Quinia wasn't standing there. "Fuck up with you? Mira got that ass on a tight ass leash."

"Nah, nothing like that. A nigga been trying to spend more time with the family."

"Feel that." I nodded.

That nigga needed to sit his ass down somewhere. He had Miracle thinking that they were gonna be together and shit, plus, Mira had been on his case about being home more, so I knew my nigga was stressing the fuck out. He was doing the right thing though. Mira was a down ass chick, and she stuck with that nigga when he ain't have shit, and he loved her; he said so himself.

"Lala still ain't fucking with you?"

"Nah, but that shit about to change as soon as four o'clock hit. I'ma be right in her line at Walmart. Either she gon' talk to me or won't nobody get no fucking service today." Lake started laughing.

"You wild, boy." We dapped up.

"You gon' do all of that because yo' best friend won't talk to you?" Quinia frowned up her pretty face. "You sure y'all ain't fucking?" I hopped off the green box and walked up in her face and glared down at her.

My tall frame towered over her short one, so she had to look up at me. My nose flared because I was trying my best not to blow the fuck up on her. But the bitch just didn't know when to fucking stop. I was tired of her questioning me about Lala—hell, about anything I did for that matter.

"I'ma say this shit slow enough for your dumb ass to understand it." I squatted a little so that I was eye level with her. "You ain't my bitch. The only thing I care about when it comes to you is whether you gon' spit or swallow. Don't fucking worry about what the fuck I do outside of tickling your tonsils. I ain't about to keep saying this shit to you. You about to piss me off, and I can promise you it won't end good for you. You got that shit?" She smacked her lips and darted her eyes in the direction of Lake who was dying laughing.

"Why you al—" she started up. I grabbed her jaws and squeezed until tears formed in the corners of her eyes.

"What the fuck I just said didn't warrant a response. Just nod yo' head that you understand." She just stared at me, so I squeezed harder. She tried to jerk away, but the more she jerked, the tighter my grip became. "You got that shit?" Her already chinky eyes became slits as she nodded her head.

I let her go, and she took a few steps back to create some distance between us. I chuckled, because if looks could kill, she would be shooting hollow points at a nigga through her eyes. She must have thought she was scaring somebody, but it was comical to me, especially with the red marks on her cheeks from my fingers.

Finally turning around and going on about her got damn business, I turned to Lake, and we both laughed. I wasn't in the business of putting my hands on bitches, but her ass was getting out of hand, and I had to show her I wasn't fucking playing with her.

I never understood why she thought she had any rights to me. I never gave her any reason to think that I wanted more than a fuck from her. She got the dick and ran with it, following me around and addressing bitches that I was talking to like she was my girl. So what had just happened was very necessary.

"Aight, nigga. I gotta go catch this stubborn ass girl." I dabbed him up. "Stay the fuck out of trouble, and don't forget we got that shit tomorrow."

"Fuck, I forgot about that shit. I told Mira we would take the kids to Defy Gravity. Fuck!"

"Don't sweat it. Ain't shit I can't move by myself. We just gotta find out the new drop." I shrugged. "And I'ma have to cuss Mitch bitch ass out about me fucking Lil' Jay's bitch ass up." I laughed.

"You finally caught up with that muthafucka?" Lake asked, looking in his phone.

"Hell yeah, and that nigga took off running behind the buildings; pissed me off when he hit the path, knowing my ass got asthma and shit." He laughed harder. "That shit ain't funny, nigga." I grabbed my chest, remembering how tight my shit got, and that nigga laughed harder. "Fuck you, nigga. I'm out."

I walked to my Tahoe and hopped in, but not before I threw Lake a bird. He laughed again before walking toward Miracle's building. I shook my head. If Lala knew that shit was going down, she would be in both of their asses. It wasn't my business, so I let him do him. I just hoped it didn't blow up in his face later.

~

"Thank you, and have a good day." Lala smiled at the customer that was currently in her line. Her line was empty, and she went to wipe her register down, but my hand covered hers the minute she started. She looked up at me with wide eyes.

"Nice to see you too." I slid my hands in my pocket and glared at her. I wanted her to know that this meeting was nowhere near pleasant. I was pissed, and if she didn't say what I wanted her to say, I was gon' make sure that she was pissed too.

"Hey, Heart. What you doing here?" She tried to play it off like shit was okay, and that further pissed me off.

"Do you really wanna make me mad, Lala?" I reached over the counter and turned off her light so no one else would come over here.

"You can't do that. You're gonna get me fired," she said in a hushed tone.

"Do it look like I give a fuck about any of that, Lala!" I purposely raised my voice. "Had yo' stubborn ass answered your phone or came to the door when I stopped by, I wouldn't be here right now. So as far as I am concerned, this..." I waved my hand around the store. "...is not my problem—it's yours."

"Heart, what do you want me to say?"

"I want you to tell me what the fuck is up. That night at the party, you were on some other shit." I knew I had an attitude about her talking to Mitch and taking money from that nigga, but she flipped on my ass like I was in the wrong. I was in my feelings when I said she could do what she wanted to, and she should've known that; she knew me.

"I was on some other shit?" She rolled her eyes. "You were the one. I don't want to do this right now. I can stop by after work, Heart." She looked around to see if anyone was watching our exchange, and that was pissing me off, so I slammed my hand down on the counter, and she jumped. "What the fuck, Heart!"

"Talk to me, got damn it!" I yelled loud enough to gain a small audience. "How I go from seeing you every fucking day to barely even talking to you?"

"You gave me away like I wasn't shit, Heart," she whined. It was moments like this that let her age show.

"Nah, you were supposed to stay the fuck away from him like I told you to." I pointed at her. We were interrupted by her boss coming over to where we were. I looked, and it was a customer of mine. I chuckled when he realized who I was.

"Ah, is everything okay, Laurence?" He looked from me to her and then back to me.

"Yeah, he's leaving. Sorry, Bailey."

"Nah, B. I ain't going no fucking where until she tells me

85

what the fuck I want to hear." My nose flared. I was trying to calm the fuck down, but Lala was making it hard. I didn't know why this meant so much to me, but it did, and I went with it.

"Do you need a few minutes? If so, that's okay." He smiled at Lala, and she nodded her head in embarrassment. She took off her smock and laid it on the register then stomped off like a little kid.

Dropping my head, I sighed deeply before I took off after her. Shit was about to get difficult as fuck; I could feel it. When we got outside, she stopped at the door, and I walked ahead of her to my truck and unlocked the doors. For a solid minute, we sat there in an uncomfortable silence.

"Lala, what the fuck is happening?" I ran my hands down my face and let them rest there while I waited on her response.

"Just the way you pretty much told Mitch he could have me made me feel like you didn't give a damn about me."

"You know that shit ain't true. I was just fucked up over the fact of that nigga giving you money and shit like I don't take care of you."

"It wasn't like that. I've said that shit more times than I care to, and I'm not gon' explain that shit again." She raised her voice and crossed her arms across her chest, causing my eyes to focus on her breasts that were spilling out of that tight ass shirt.

"Aight, damn." I brought my eyes back up to hers. "I just know how that nigga work, and I don't want that for you," I said honestly. Again, the car fell silent, and Lala was staring straight ahead. I could tell that she was trying to figure out what to say next.

"Why do you care?" She was barely audible. If the car wasn't so quiet, I wouldn't have heard her. Her eyes were focused on something outside. I followed them but couldn't figure out what it was.

"What the fuck do you mean, why do I care, Lala? You know how I feel about you." I was burning a hole in the side of her face.

"How do you feel about me?" I didn't know how to take her question, so I kept it safe.

"You know I look at you like family. I wanna make sure you good. I love you, you know that shit, so I don't know where all that shit is coming from." Her eyes finally met mine, and a lone tear rolled down her cheek.

"What if I want more?" Her stare didn't waiver, and neither did mine. She had caught me by surprise, and I didn't know what to say. I knew what I felt, but I also knew that I wasn't good for her, so I didn't process the feelings. Her saying that put me in a weird position. "Wow!" she said when I didn't say anything.

She gave me another look before she climbed out of my truck and shut the door, but she was still looking at me through my tinted windows. She didn't say anything else though; she just turned around and walked back into Walmart.

What the fuck just happened? This shit had me all fucked up. A part of me wanted to run after her and tell her that I wanted her ass too, but then the other part of me didn't want to fuck up her life and our friendship. Although after today, our friendship would never be the same. A nigga was fucked up right now, and I needed to think about this shit.

MIRACLE

$\mathcal{I}$ was going over my information for my state test that was coming up. I had just finished all of my hours for cosmetology school. Unlike my mother, I wanted to do something with myself outside of live off the government. I wasn't downing that shit, because food stamps were the reason I was as thick as I was, but I wanted more for me.

My mind drifted to Lake, who I hadn't seen nor heard from in over a week. That wasn't like him. I knew he had a girl, but he would always make time for me... always. Lake loved me, and I knew that much, regardless of what anyone else thought.

After the whole Waffle House fiasco, he came by a few days later and explained that the girl he dissed me for was just somebody he used to sleep around with. He said it was nothing and promised me that it was over. The way the chick acted made me feel like it was more than what he said it was, but I gave him the benefit of the doubt. With his current disappearing act, he clearly didn't deserve that.

I told him that I refused to share him with anyone other than Mira. It sounded crazy, but I did it for him. I knew that my role in his life was more significant than hers, so I allowed it. He said that it made life easier for him, and that's what I was here to do. It was becoming harder and harder to accept, but I knew our time was coming.

He always told me that he was going to leave her, but he wanted to make sure that his kids were straight and stable, and I believed him. The bond we had was more than just sex; it was more than people would ever know. I was his rider, and he knew that, so if he needed time, I would give him that.

My front door being unlocked pulled me out of my thoughts, and I turned toward the door. Only two people had access to my house, and I knew Lala was at work. The minute his cologne assaulted my nose, I went in defense mode. I loved him, but that didn't mean he could disappear when he wanted to.

"Where have you been, Lake? You aren't answering my calls, and I haven't seen you in over a week. What the fuck!" I yelled, jumping in his face.

"You better chill the fuck out, Miracle, before you piss me the fuck off." He slightly pushed me out of the way and headed back to my bedroom without answering any of my questions. He was not about to get off that easily, so I headed right back there with him.

Standing in the doorway of my bedroom, I watched as he stripped down to nothing and laid across my bed, staring up at the ceiling. I couldn't help but admire his body. He had an athletic build that drove me crazy when he worked in and out of me when we were making love. Lake was sexy, and he knew it.

"So where you been? With that other hoe?" I said, referring to the chick that popped up at the Waffle House that night of DLo's party.

"Don't start that shit, Miracle. We talked about this shit."

"Is this how shit gon' go tonight? Me asking questions and you telling me not to start? 'Cause if it is, you can fucking leave." I pointed at the door, knowing I didn't mean any of it. The way he was staring at me made me take a step back. I thought he was about to get his clothes, but he bypassed them and walked right over to me.

Without saying a word, he snatched the shirt that I had on violently and caused all of the buttons that were on it to fall to the floor. He started to snatch the shirt off my shoulders, and I tried to jerk away. He grabbed my chin and bore into my eyes while he pulled down my leggings and thongs. Once I matched his nakedness, he backed me up against the wall and looked down at me.

"Are you gon' say something or just walk around here like a fucking psycho?"

Again, I didn't get a response. He just picked me up by my legs, slamming my back against the wall. Reaching down between us, he grabbed his dick and placed it at my opening and forced his way into my goodies.

The way he pumped in and out of me was like he was trying to show me something or make a point. His pace was fast, and my titties bounced to the beat of his frustration. Grabbing my neck and shoving his tongue down my throat, I tried to keep up, but he was on some other shit. I didn't know what to think.

Sex with us was always good, but he was fucking me like I was some kinda hoe, not a woman he loved. I wanted to cuss his ass out, but my body betrayed me, and a powerful orgasm took over.

"Ohhh fuckkkkk," I moaned out as my body shook with pleasure. I was in such a state of bliss that I was unable to close my mouth, so it just hung open, causing him to chuckle.

"You're supposed to be my peace," he said as he continued to pound my pussy like it owed him something. "I don't want to argue when I come here." He clenched his teeth. "I get that shit everywhere else. I'm stressed the fuck out, and I came here to get peace. Fuck!" I could tell that he was almost at his peak and was about to bring me to another one. "Stop stressing a nigga out with shit that don't matter. Ah, fuck yeah!"

"Shit, shit, shit, shit, shit!" I panted as he sped up and brought me to another orgasm. "Babbbbyyyyyyy!" I moaned out.

"Ummhmmm," he grunted, and then filled my womb up with all of his seeds.

I secretly hoped like hell that one of them little bastards found one of my eggs so I could house one of his babies, we never used protection and I ran out of birth control pills months ago. He didn't know that, and I ain't plan on telling him either.

He pumped into me a few more times before he pulled out and lowered me to the ground. My legs were weak, so I stumbled, and he had to catch me. He picked me back up and carried me to the bed. I laid on my back and he laid down beside me.

"I'm sorry." My response was breathily. He chuckled but that's it. That's all I got. In the next few minutes, all I heard was snoring. I wanted to be mad, but to be honest, I was just glad that he was here. I slid over to where he was and laid my head on his chest and got some much-needed rest myself.

I was awakened by his phone blaring. I knew it wasn't his girl because she had a special ringtone. I knew that because when I heard that, I was to be quiet. He hardly ever answered, but when he did, I knew my role.

Raising up and looking at his phone, I noticed a number that wasn't saved. I shook my head and was about to lay back down once it stopped ringing, but a text came through, and my curiosity got the best of me, and I looked. I was happy that he hadn't blocked them from showing up on his lock screen.

704-555-6789: Lake you were supposed to be here by now and my pussy misses you.

I picked up the phone and looked at the message. Pissed was an understatement. I wanted to stab his ass. I turned to where he was laying and met his menacing stare. I jumped and dropped his phone on the ground.

"Find what the fuck you were looking for?" He sat up, never taking his eyes off of me. I just stood there like a deer in head-lights. "Do I go through your shit?" he questioned through gritted teeth.

"Who is she?" I asked well below a whisper.

"What!" he yelled, and I jumped.

"Who is she!" I matched his tone. "Is it her?"

He dropped his head and chuckled, but it wasn't an amusing laugh; it was damn near demented. I took a few steps back to create some space between us. Sighing heavily, he reached down and picked up his phone. He read the message and ran his hand down his face then laid back down on the bed. He was stressed, and whoever that was on the phone was the reason.

"What's up, Lake?" I asked, truly concerned. He sat up just as fast as he laid down. Without saying a word, he got dressed and grabbed his keys and phone and left. He didn't even bother to wash his ass. I didn't know what the fuck was going on with him, but I didn't like it.

I laid on the couch and called him back to back, and when he didn't answer, I bawled my eyes out. I felt like I was losing him, and I didn't want that.

LALA

"Wow," I said to myself as I thought about the conversation I had with Heart earlier. He just blew me off. I couldn't believe he just sat there. I guess I was fooling myself thinking that he wanted what I wanted out of this. He was just my best friend, and that's all he wanted. I guess I needed to find a way to come to grips with that.

It was time for me to get off, and I didn't want to ask anyone to take me home because I didn't feel like talking, so I decided on an Uber. After I clocked out, I went and stood outside and grabbed my phone so that I could order one, when a deep voice called my name.

"Lala!" I turned around and was face to face with Mitch.

"Hey, Mitch. How are you?" I tried to keep it short. He had gotten me into enough shit. I continued on my phone.

"You never did say when you were gon' let me take you out."

"Um, I don't think that's a good idea." I looked up at him for the first time. The man was sexy, no doubt, but he was bad news, and I was starting to see just how bad.

"Why, because Heart said so?"

"No, because you're married, and I plan on doing that one day. You can't really do that with someone that already has those papers, now can you?" I tilted my head to the side.

"That can be taken care of," he countered, and I laughed.

"Yep, they all say that. Nah, playa, I'm good. I believe in Karma, and I want no parts of her." I stood up straight and stretched, and that was a bad idea, because his eyes were on my breasts in no time. I cleared my throat, and he chuckled.

Shaking my head, I couldn't help but smile because he knew what kinda nigga he was, which is why he laughed. He knew he wasn't shit. I was about to dismiss myself, but Heart's Tahoe came flying up. I just put my head down because I already knew how this shit looked. What the fuck! Could this really be happening right now?

He rolled down the window, and the look on his face was stone cold. He was pissed, and there was no denying it. I wanted to clear up any confusion that this scene may have caused, but Heart didn't give me a chance to do that.

"I came to get you so we could talk, but I see you got a ride!" He shook his head and rolled up the window.

"Heart, it's not like that. I—" I started, but he pulled off before I could finish. "Fuck!"

Was he coming to talk about the possibility of us being together? Did he think about what we talked about earlier? Did he feel the same way I did? Why didn't he just say that earlier? Fuck! What just happened?

"Damn, he was mad as fuck." Mitch laughed. I shot him a look that said go away. "Hey, don't be mad at me. I just came to pick some milk up for the house and seen you out looking all tired and shit. I stopped to talk. Nothing more and nothing less."

"Mm hmm." I started to walk off from him, but he kept on with his shit.

"I can take you home though." He grinned.

"No thank you." I snarled and walked off to call an Uber. He had caused enough drama in my life, and I wasn't having it. I needed to hurry up and get to Heart's so I could talk to him about what he thought he saw. I knew he was tired of hearing me say that it wasn't like that, but it really wasn't.

~

*A*fter I got home, I showered really quick and put on a cute little PINK shorts outfit and a pair of pink and white Air Max to match. Once I threw my hair in a ponytail, I headed out to see if I could get Heart to talk to me.

Walking to the bottom of the Creek, I could see that the green box was full of niggas and little hoes waiting to get some attention from these dealers. I just hoped that Heart wasn't occupied because I would hate to have to act a fool out here. He was gonna talk to me whether he liked that or not.

"Uh, aye, Lala, what you doing down here?" Lake greeted

me, his demeanor was letting me know that I was not about to like what I was walking into.

"Where's Heart, and don't bullshit me?" I glared at him, and his eyes darted back and forth, so I knew he was about to lie.

"He bounced for a few."

"Lying ass. Both his cars here, and his paranoid ass don't trust no one to drive for him but you and me, and we both right here." I shrugged, and he dropped his head, and I walked around him. "That's fucked up," I threw over my shoulder.

"Lala, you know it ain't like that. I don't know what the fuck y'all two got going on, but y'all need to fix that shit. 'Cause both of y'all bipolar asses getting on my got damn nerves!" he yelled after me. I guess he realized where I was going because he started to try and stop me. "Hol' up, wait."

Before he could get to me, I was opening the door to Heart's apartment and walking in on the Quinia bitch giving him head. His head was thrown back like he was enjoying the shit. I didn't know what came over me, but I picked up the ashtray on the end table near the door and hauled it at his head. When it crashed against the wall, he reached for his gun and pointed it at me. When he noticed that it was me, he lowered it and pushed Quinia to the floor.

It was in his best interest not to come anywhere near me. He stood up to pull up his pants and looked everywhere in his apartment but at me. I stood there with my hands on my hips, waiting for him to say something.

"I know you ain't about to do this right now 'cause this bitch walked in the door," Quinia said, getting up off the floor.

"Oh fuck!" I heard Lake say from the door.

I gave that bitch just enough time to get her bearing, and I ran over and popped that bitch in the mouth. She swung and hit me on the side of the face, but I didn't feel it. I was that mad. I just kept swinging. I was trying to take her fucking head off. She somehow slipped and went to the ground. I hopped on top of her and tried to fuck her life all the way up. I was filled with aggression, and I needed someone to take that shit out on, and she was the perfect candidate.

"Chill, La," I heard Heart say as he was pulling me off her. He finally pried my hands off from around her hair, and he lifted me in the air.

"Get your fucking hands off of me." I kicked and hit him all in his back until he placed me on my feet. As soon as he did, I turned to face him and rocked the shit out of him. I couldn't even explain why I was so mad; I just knew that I was. I started out the door, and Lake grabbed me up to try and calm me down, making me struggle against his strong hold. "Let me go!" I screamed on him, and he threw his hands up in the air in surrender, and I walked out the door mad as hell.

I could hear that bitch in there running her mouth and Heart telling her to get the fuck out. I already knew that he was on his way after me, but I wasn't going home. I took off toward the top of the Creek, but I kept going. I needed time to think, and I wasn't in the mood to deal with anybody's shit.

The night air was just right. It was nearing fall, my favorite time of year. I didn't need a jacket, but I wasn't sweating either. I could feel my phone vibrating in my bra where I had put it on my way down to Heart's. I didn't bother to look and see who it was, because it was one of two people, and I didn't want to hear from anybody right now.

Walking in the dark calmed me. I wasn't worried about nobody fucking with me because even though my dad was dead, his name still meant something around here. I walked until I felt myself relax; only then did I turn around and head back home.

I was right around the corner from the apartments when I noticed a Mercedes turn the corner. It slowed down when it got to where I was. I kept walking. I didn't know who it was, so I wasn't about to stop.

"Aye, lil' mean ass, slow down," I heard Mitch say from the driver seat. It caused me to speed up even more, because the way I saw it, he was the reason for all of my turmoil at this present moment. I heard him put the car in park and get out of the car, but my pace didn't waver. "Yo, Lala, wait! A nigga just trying to make sure you good."

"I'm great. Thanks for asking. I just wanna be left alone."

"Yo' little young ass shouldn't be walking out here alone." His tone was disgusting, and he was starting to further piss me off. "Let me take you home." Finally catching up with me, he grabbed my arm to stop my stride. I jerked away. "Whoa!" he threw his hands up.

"Look, it's been a long night, and I just want to be by myself." I looked at him, pleading with my eyes, but this dumb ass licked his lips like he didn't hear anything I just said. "You know what..." I threw my hands up and walked away before I went off.

I got a full two steps before he grabbed my arm again, and I tried to snatch away, but he gripped me tighter.

"Could you please let me go." The look in his eyes was sinister, and at that moment, I regretted ever speaking to him.

"You think you gon' act like that toward me when I laced your ungrateful ass? Huh?" he said through gritted teeth.

"I never asked you for shit." I finally shook loose from his grasp.

"But you took it and spent that shit though." He chuckled.

"Hey, I tried to give it back, and you wouldn't take it, so don't make it like I needed anything from you." I was getting pissed off, and if this conversation didn't end soon, I was sure that it was gonna take a turn for the worse.

"You just like these other little whores around here, just chasing money and dick," he spat and then turned around to get in his car. I should've left well enough alone, but my pride and attitude wouldn't let me. So I followed him toward his car, running my mouth when I should have just kept walking.

"And you are just like all these other bitch ass niggas around here, who running around here thinking they God's gift when really they ain't shit." My chest heaved up and down. "I bet ya wife don't fucking know you out here fucking everything that moves. I wonder what the fuck she would say then."

The look he gave me told me that I should have ran, and when my body caught up with my mind, he already had his hands around my throat.

"Was that a threat, you little bitch?" I struggled against his hold. "Since you got so much mouth, let me show you what I do to little bitches like you," he said, lifting me off the ground by my neck and toward his car. When we reached the car, he tried to throw me in the back seat. That's when I freaked the hell out. I knew that if he got me in that car, he was gonna rape me; there was no doubt in my mind.

Reaching up, I tried to claw his face, but he put a tighter grip on my neck. I was starting to lose consciousness, but I knew if I did, it was over for me. I did what my dad always told me to do in a time like this. I kneed that muthafucka in the balls as hard as I could. He immediately went down, and as soon as his hands was off of me, I took off toward the Creek. This had been one hell of a night.

HEART

"She ain't fucking with you, bruh." Lake laughed, and I wanted to punch him in the mouth. I wasn't in the mood to joke around right now.

I was still trying to figure out what the fuck happened. When I saw Mitch out there in her face at her job, a nigga got pissed off. After we talked in my car, I knew I owed her some kind of explanation for not saying shit, so I went back to holla at her. Lo and behold, this nigga was sitting there all in her got damn face.

Mitch was starting to piss me the fuck off. He was being shady as shit with the product and prices. And now he was trying to fuck up Lala's life, and I wasn't about to let that happen. I'd kill him first, and I wasn't in the mood for a fucking war with that nigga.

"Shit, you know how Lala is. Maybe she took off walking." He shrugged, seeing I wasn't with the bullshit.

"How you gon' let that bitch do this to my sister's face?" Lanae came tearing across the parking lot dragging Quinia behind her. I didn't bother to answer her because I didn't feel the need to. I didn't owe her shit, and her sister ran her got damn mouth too much, so she got what she had coming. However, I didn't expect for Lala to react like that. She shocked the shit out of me.

Shit was changing between us overnight. As bad as I wanted to fight it, a part of me knew that she was the one for me. My only fear was that I would fuck it up before we got to really explore what we both knew was fate.

"Yo, get the fuck away from here with that shit," Lake said, stepping in front of her before she could get to my car.

"Move, Lake. If that nigga can fuck my sister, he should damn sure be able to protect her."

"Yo' sister got too much fucking mouth. She been fucking with that girl since forever. So when Lala put them paws on her, it was justified." Lake chuckled and shrugged.

"So you think it's okay to let her get jumped?"

"Jumped!" me and Lake yelled at the same time.

"Ain't nobody jump her dumb ass. She was sucking my dick, and Lala walked in and went the fuck off. She ain't need no help, trust me," I finally spoke up, but something caught my eye at the top. It looked like Lala running down the sidewalk. I headed in that direction but was stopped by Lanae running up and pulling my shirt.

"No, muthafucka. You gon' explain this shit."

I grabbed her arm and twisted it behind her back until she

cried out in pain and then I pulled a little more. The fucked-up part about this whole situation was I was knocking her ass down too. So more than likely, she was more concerned about why Lala did what she did versus what actually happened to her sister.

"You know better than to fucking touch me without my permission," I said through gritted teeth and close to her ear.

"Why would Lala do that to my sister if you ain't fucking her!" she cried out.

"That's your fucking problem now. You worried about what the fuck I'm doing with Lala. That's the only reason you brought your ass over here. I bet your fucking sister don't know I knocked ya ass down two days ago though, now do she? Worry about that shit!"

"What the fuck, Lanae!" I heard Quinia say.

I didn't stay around to see the festivities. I headed to the top of the Creek so I could go and see if it was Lala I saw running down the sidewalk. When I got to her building, I saw Mitch pulling in like a bat out of hell. I stood on the rail leading to her building. He slowly rode by, and when he saw me, he rolled down the window. I could tell that he was pissed off, and I wondered if it had anything to do with Lala.

"'Sup, nigga?" he asked.

"Not shit." I kept it short and sweet. He looked at me and then the building.

"Aight, holla at ya tomorrow." He threw me a head nod and headed on out the same way he came in. That shit didn't feel right to me. Why the fuck was she running when he was pulling into her section like he had a problem?

Once he was out of eyesight, I took the stairs two at a time. I didn't know what I was about to say or how this little meeting was about to go. She was a hot head and so was I, but we were talking whether either of us wanted it or not. We had to figure this shit out.

I hated the weirdness that our relationship had taken on. Things used to be so fucking chill with us. Now it was like we were walking on eggshells around each other. That wasn't us, and we needed to fix that shit and fast. I was just worried about what it would take to fix it and if it was the right thing to do.

Walking up to her door, I could hear her crying, and that sent off alarms. Something was telling me that Mitch had something to do with her tears, and I wasn't feeling it. I banged on the door, and she got quiet. I could still hear her moving around.

"Open the got damn door, Lala," I said, letting her know that it was me.

When she opened the door, I walked in, and she fell into my arms and broke down. Moving enough to shut the door and lock it, I grabbed her shoulders and pulled her away from me so that I could take a good look at her. I needed to make sure that she was okay. The second I saw the marks on her neck, I could feel my body heat up.

Picking her up, I carried her to the couch and sat her on my lap in the straddling position. I knew that probably wasn't the best idea, but at this point, I didn't give a fuck. I just wanted to make sure that she was okay.

"What happened?" My voice was laced with anger, but I was trying my best to stay calm, but it was fucking hard.

"I wasn't with him, Heart. He came to my job as I was leaving. I didn't ask him to come," she said through her tears. I could barely make out what she was saying, but I got the gist of it.

"I don't give a fuck about that shit, Laurence! What the fuck happened to your neck, and don't lie to me?" I laid her head on my chest with her face facing the door. I looked down and took in the bruises. The more I looked, the more pissed I got. If Mitch did this shit, we were definitely gonna have some fucking problems, and I had a bad feeling this was all him. "La, talk to me, baby."

I wrapped my hands around her waist while she cried into my chest. Something about this felt so right; like this was where she was supposed to be minus the fucking bruises on her neck. Rubbing my hand up and down her back, trying to sooth her, I got her to finally calm down enough to look back at me.

"After I caught you and Quinia, I knew that you would come looking for me, so I took off walking so that I could calm down. On my way back to the apartments, Mitch stopped me and tried to talk to me, but I told him I didn't feel like it, and I asked him to leave me alone. He basically said I owed him a—"

"Did he—"

"No!" she blurted out quickly. "But he tried!" She looked into my eyes. I grinded my teeth, trying not to spaz because I told her that the nigga was grimy as fuck. "He got mad because I was talking shit to him, so he choked me out and tried to throw me in the car, but I kicked him in the nuts and got away." She broke down again into my chest.

"Don't even worry about that shit. I'll take care of that," I said it with so much conviction that it caused her to sit up and stare into my eyes.

"Please no. Just leave it alone."

"No can do." My hands dropped down and rested on her ass. I don't know why or how, but that's where they landed, and the shit felt good, so I wasn't about to move them, and she didn't ask me to. "That's why I told yo' ass to stay the hell away from him. He a dirty ass muthafucka. I wasn't saying that shit for no fucking reason, Lala. Now that nigga think you owe him something. How much he give you?" I said that, and she started crying again. She was just gon' have to take that shit, because I wasn't holding nothing in.

"Three," she lifted her head and said.

"Bet!" I was gonna give his fucking money back right after I rocked the shit out of him for putting his fucking hands on her like that. *Pussy ass nigga.*

"Can you get your phone," Lala said with an attitude and tried to get up, but I held her in place. That little movement had my shit growing, and I couldn't control it. Like I said, this felt right, and I guess my dick agreed.

"Don't worry about my phone; that shit ain't important." I grabbed her chin and made her look at me. Damn this girl was beautiful. There was an innocence about her that drew me in, and our connection was undeniable, so this made sense. I just didn't know if I was ready for it. "What's up with that shit earlier?"

Her eyes took on a sadness that made me feel like shit for leaving her hanging. I just needed to figure out the right way to go about it. I didn't want to go off emotions, because I already knew how that would go. I needed to think this through; our relationship was counting on it.

"Nothing." She smacked her lips. "It's not even important."

"Stop acting like a fucking brat, Laurence, and fucking talk to me." I raised my voice unintentionally. I closed my eyes and sighed heavily to try and calm down. I hated when she got like this with her little stubborn ass. "This shit ain't easy for me, Lala, and you know it. I love yo' little ass, and I don't wanna do shit to fuck up the relationship that we got, so I need to move smart. I had to think. I couldn't just lay that shit out right then and there. Ain't shit I can do about that—take it or fucking leave it."

"I want more," she said just above a whisper, her eyes focused on everything in the room but me. I grabbed her jaws and forced her to look at me. "I've tried just being Lala, the friend, but I don't know if I can do that anymore." The air became thick. I knew what my heart wanted, but my mind was telling me that this could possibly fuck up a lot. I didn't know if I was ready to take that chance or not.

"I'm no good for you, La," I said honestly. As bad as I wished that was a lie, it wasn't. I was in the streets; that was how I lived, and I didn't have any plans on changing that shit anytime soon. It was all I knew. I wouldn't know what to do if she got hurt because of me. "You deserve better than me."

"No, you're wrong. I deserve you, Heart! No one will ever love me like you, and vice versa. You know me better than I know myself. My heart craves you," she said with tears dancing around the rim of her eye. "Do you have any idea what it's like to compare every man I come across to you? Or watching you with bitch after bitch, knowing I was supposed to be the one in your arms, your bed, and most importantly your heart." I shivered at her words. A nigga ain't never been one to be giddy, but she was warming a nigga up.

What Lala didn't know was that I loved her from the moment I saw her sitting on the stoop crying when her dad died. I knew the shit sounded suspect as hell, but it was the truth. I wasn't no pervert or no shit like that. What I felt for her back then wasn't sexual; it was a connection from my soul. I knew she was gonna be a permanent fixture in my life. I just didn't want to fuck that up, and I knew I would... Somehow, I would.

"You know how a nigga feel about you, Lala, but—"

"No buts." She cut me off. "Just let it be that! Heart, I'm grown, and I can take care of myself. I just want us..." She pointed back and forth between the two of us. "...to be."

I dropped my head. My heart was winning the battle that it was having with my mind and will power. She put her little pointy ass finger under my chin and lifted my head so we were eye level. I stared deep in her eyes, and I could feel the love she had for a nigga, and I knew what I was feeling at that moment was real.

"Move ya pointy ass fucking nail." I mugged her, and she just stared at me. "And if you ever put your hands on me again, I'ma fuck you up."

"Are you fucking serious, Heart?" she said, smacking her lips and trying to get up. "Stop, let me go. I'm trying to be serious, and you being a asshole." She struggled against me as I held her in place.

Something came over me, and I crashed my lips against hers. The electricity that flowed through that kiss was indescribable. It was something that I never felt before. Grabbing the back of her neck, my tongue parted her lips and went exploring. The kiss was so deep and passionate that my eyes closed involuntarily.

Things heated up quickly. It wasn't until I felt her grinding against my dick did my eyes come open. I gave her a warning look without breaking the kiss, and she just smiled against my lips. The line was already crossed; I just hoped that we were making the right decision.

I grabbed the bottom of her shirt that she had on and lifted it over her head. I undid her bra, and her perky titties sat up like they were fake, but I knew for a fact that they were all natural. She bit down on her bottom lip as I rolled her nipple between my index finger and thumb, causing her to grind harder on my dick and a slight moan to escape my lips.

"You sure about this?" I asked, pulling her toward me and connecting with her lips again. She nodded while reaching down to unbuckle my pants. I gave her one more warning look and pressed her lips against mine.

I stood up, and her legs found their rightful place around my waist. All that could be heard through her apartment was panting and moaning. I tapped her thighs, and she slid down until her feet were on the ground. I stared down at her, and she chewed on her bottom lip.

"I love yo' stubborn ass," I told her, meaning every word.

"I love yo' mean ass too."

I chuckled and sat down on the couch in front of her. I slid two fingers in the waistband of her shorts and slid them down, exposing her greatness. She stepped out of her shorts and thongs and kicked them out of the way. For a minute, I just stood back and looked at how sexy she was. Her blemish free skin glowed under the dim light of the lamp she had in her living room. Her body was sick, especially naked. I grabbed the back of her legs and pulled her to me.

I could tell that she was nervous because her breathing had picked up, and she was slightly shaking. We were about to take a big ass step—one that we couldn't come back from. As much as I dreamed of this moment, I tried to prevent it just as much. I was here now, and I was about to make it a night to remember.

I grabbed her right leg and threw it over my shoulder. She was so damn short that I had to lean down just a little to get to where I needed to be. I flicked my tongue across her clit, and she jumped. I grabbed her ass to keep her in place. I ran my tongue the length of her slit, and she was wet as hell all fucking ready. My shit was on brick.

"Mmmmm," she moaned out as I nibbled on her clit. "Fuck, Heart."

I smiled because I was teasing her. I hadn't even put no work in. I didn't know what kinda fuck nigga she'd been fucking with, but I was about to show her why she waited for me.

Covering her pussy with my mouth, I lightly sucked while swirling my tongue around her clit. Grabbing my head, she started to grind on my face. I sucked, nibbled, and licked until she was filling up my mouth with her nectar.

"Oh my God, shittttttt," she cried out.

I made sure not to leave anything behind. Once I licked her clean, I looked up at her and she looked dazed.

"You ain't tapping out on me, are you?" She bit her lip and pushed me back on the couch. I raised my ass so that she could get my pants off. When they were off, she mounted my lap and leaned down to taste herself on my lips.

My dick poked at her opening like he knew that was home. She tooted her ass up to give him the access that he was demanding. Once the head was in, she slowly bounced, trying to take all of me in. I could tell that she was struggling against my size; the pain was etched on her face.

"You good, La?"

"Ummhmmm." She bit her lip once she reached the base. I had to try and divert my attention somewhere else before I came prematurely. It was cliché as fuck, but my dick fit her perfectly. It was like her pussy was designed to house me, and I loved it. She was wet as hell and warm just like I liked it.

Slowly rocking back and forth, the pain on her face slowly faded, and it was replaced with pure bliss. The more I stretched her, the harder she rocked her hips.

"Fuck... you feel good," I said as I kissed the bruises on her neck. "Do that shit." I slapped her ass.

She leaned up and looked me in the eyes as she placed her hands on my chest for leverage and started bouncing up and down while moving her hips in a circular motion. You could hear her wetness; that shit was a turn on in itself.

"Oh my God, Heart. I'm gonna cum."

"Shit, come on then." I egged her on. I held on to her hips as she continued to work the hell out of my dick. "Damn, La.

"Ah shit! Oh fuck." She shut her eyes tight as she concentrated on getting hers. I decided to help her out. I lifted my hips and thrust into her from underneath, matching her thrust for thrust. "Yes, yes, yes, baby, fuck, yes!" she screamed, and I felt her coat my dick with her greatness. "Ahhh shit." Her body shook as she collapsed onto my chest, still slowly rocking her hips, making sure that she rode every minute of that wave.

I gave her a minute to get herself together. I wanted to show her a few things, and I couldn't do that on this couch. When her breathing returned back to normal, I stood up, still inside of her, heading back to her room. I had never been in here, but the apartments were made the same.

When I reached her room, I lowered her onto the bed then leaned down and kissed her lips. I spread her legs and took my thumb and applied pressure to her clit as I started to move in and out of her. She was still wet as fuck. I looked down and watched as I moved in and out of her. I had never been so in tuned with a woman's body as I was right now with Lala, and it made it that much better.

"This shit gon' have to work, Lala. I don't think I can take anybody else feeling what the fuck I'm feeling right now." I leaned down and kissed her again. She gave me a lazy smile.

"It's me and you, right?" she said breathily.

"Yeah, baby; me and you," I said and started to move in and out of her at an even pace. I meant what I said, and I was going to do what I needed to do to keep my lifestyle away from her. I just prayed that we made the right decision. I spread her legs and grinded into her to let her know just how serious I was.

"Ahhhh God, yes!" she moaned out. We made love until the wee hours of the morning, and I must say, I had definitely been missing out.

I was gonna make this shit right. First thing I needed to do was handle Mitch's bitch ass.

MITCH

I couldn't believe that little bitch. I should've strangled the fuck out of her. She didn't know who the fuck she was messing with. I could almost bet my life she called that nigga Heart and told him what went down. That crazy muthafucka could come after me if he wanted to; I'd fuck up his whole got damn life.

The nigga was one of my best soldiers; he just had a fucking problem with authority. He was loyal though, so I couldn't get rid of him. He did what the fuck he was supposed to and made me a lot of money—him and Lake. They just weren't some get in line kinda niggas, and that made it hard for me.

Like the fact that I told that nigga that my family was off limits, and I heard that he pistol whipped my nephew, Lil' Jay. I didn't know what that nigga did, but I told him not to fuck with his unstable ass, and out of respect for me, Heart was supposed to let me handle any issues he had with him, but you see how that went down.

I'd been waiting for that nigga Heart to hit me up about the situation with Lala since last night. I hadn't heard anything yet, so I was chill. We had a party tonight at Club Mint, and I was sure he would be there. I just hoped he came there acting like he had some got damn sense.

"Boss man," Mello said, walking into my office, giving me dap. "Gilda let me in," he informed me, speaking of my maid.

"'Sup, Mello?" I dapped him back.

Mello was my nigga a hundred grand. He was my right hand and the only man I trusted enough to know my moves. Nigga been there from the beginning, helping me build my empire. Hell, he was the one that introduced me to my wife, who in turn introduced me to my connect. My loyalty was with him because his was with me.

"Shit might heat up with that nigga Heart," I confessed. He needed to know just in case shit get serious. That nigga was unpredictable. That was what made him good at what he did, but it made it hard as hell for his enemies.

"For that shit they pulled at the crib the other day?" He brought up when I asked Heart to stand down, and he refused. I talked to him about that shit, but he brushed it off as if I was the one tripping and just walked out in mid conversation. That was how I knew it was gon' be some shit.

"Nah, that little bitch he been running after and claim he ain't knocking down. She was running her mouth, and I choked her ass out," I said, giving half-truths. I didn't need to lie, especially not to Mello, but the shit was embarrassing. I had never been told no by a female in my life, and I wasn't trying to hear his shit if he knew I choked her out because she wouldn't fuck with a nigga. "And his ass ran up on Lil' Jay."

"You know how he feel about that broad." Mello chuckled, ignoring the shit about my nephew. Mello thought that I should cut ties with my nephew because he was always in some shit, but I couldn't do that. He was my blood, him and Jason.

"Don't I." We shared a laugh right before Wynn walked in the office. I looked at her dressed in designer head to toe. My wife was beautiful, from her gray eyes to the perfectly sculpted body that my hard-earned money paid for. She was the perfect trophy wife, but she was sneaky as hell. Every move she made was calculated, and I hated that shit because I felt like I had to watch myself around my own got damn wife. "Yes, Wynn?"

"Well hello to you too, dear." She came around and sat on the corner of the desk, facing me. For a minute, she just sat there and looked at me with a smirk on her face.

When I met Wynn, she was a meek, quiet girl. Somewhere along the lines, the street life got the best of her, and she lost her spark. I knew I put her through a lot, but I loved her in my own little way, and she accepted that and gave me the same love in return. Most would say that wasn't a good thing, but it worked for us. I did my thing, and she shopped and looked pretty—that was us.

"What can I do for you, beautiful?" I asked, softening my approach so she could get the fuck out and I could finish doing business with Mello.

"Hello, Mello. How are you?" she said, not bothering to turn around. Her eyes were still on me.

"Wynn," was all he said, and she giggled.

"Where are we going tonight?" she asked. I normally didn't take her with me while I was out. I didn't need her knowing what I did. Her father was my connect, and the last thing I needed was for him to try and fuck me because daddy's little girl was scorned. I didn't have time for that, and she knew it.

"We aren't going anywhere. I'm going out with the fellas." I looked into her beautiful gray eyes. "Don't you have some girl-friends to chill with or something?"

I didn't know exactly how the situation with Heart was gonna go down, so I didn't want her there and shit break out. If some-thing happened to her, I would have to explain that shit to Wyndel, her father. I wasn't prepared to do that. He was one of the most powerful men on the east coast.

"No, I don't, but I do have a husband to chill with, and that's exactly who's arm I will be attached to tonight."

The look she gave me dared me to argue with her. Good thing I didn't feel like going back and forth, so I let her have that one. I would just have to be on my best behavior tonight.

"Whatever you want, dear." I smiled, and she nodded.

"Great. I'll be ready by ten." She leaned over and pecked my lips, and even that was cold. I shook my head and watched her walk out of the room. Right before she left, she looked back. "See ya later, Mello." She giggled and walked out.

Lately, she had been super extra when Mello was around. If I didn't know any better, I would have to check him, but I knew him, and he would never. Even though I did my thing, she was still my wife, and he would never disrespect me like that.

"Something is wrong with that woman." Mello shook his head with a scowl on his face.

"Tell me about it. I'm married to her." We both shared a laugh.

We talked business for a while and chopped it up, before we parted ways to get ready for later tonight. I had a few things I needed to take care of before we headed out. I needed to make sure shit was straight in case Heart came with the bullshit. He was gon' get a rude awakening tonight.

~

The atmosphere was chill as fuck. The music was jumping, and the people were moving. I was actually enjoying myself. Wynn took her rightful place in my lap and stared on at the many patrons of Club Mist.

"Order another bottle!" I yelled over the music to Mello. He nodded and went in search of the bottle girl so he could order us another bottle of Henny. We had killed the first one we got when we arrived.

"The fuck wrong with you?" I asked when I noticed an immediate change in Wynn's demeanor.

"Nothing. I got to go to the bathroom." She stood up and tugged on the little ass dress that she had on. Her ass was barely covered, and the damn thing left nothing to the imagination. I didn't bother making her change because I didn't have the energy to argue with her, so I just dealt with the stares of the men we passed. As long as they didn't approach her, we were good.

I watched as she headed in the direction of the bathroom. I sat back in my seat and enjoyed the scenery. There was a mixture of women in attendance. Normally, I would have had me one of each.

Quite a bit of time had passed, and neither Wynn nor Mello had come back, but before the thought could cross my mind for a second time, Heart and Lake walked up into the VIP section. Heart's presence wasn't threatening or confrontational, but that didn't mean shit when it came to him. Like I said before, the nigga was unpredictable.

"Aye, what's up, nigga." I went to dap him up, but he rocked the shit out of me instead. I stumbled back and tripped over the chair that I was originally sitting in. We now had the attention of every muthafucka in the building. The DJ had even stopped spinning his record. The club wasn't that big, so commotion was easily detected. "The fuck, nigga!" I wiped my mouth that was covered in blood.

"If you ever in yo' muthafucking life put your hands on Lala again, I promise you won't live to talk about it." He stood over me with his fists balled up. I looked around trying to figure out where the hell Mello's ass was.

"I'on know what the fuck that little bitch told you but—" He cut me off with a gun to my head.

"Call her out her name again," he said through gritted teeth. I smacked his gun out of my face and glared at him. I hope he knew that he just made the biggest mistake of his life. "She spoken for, my nigga. Stay the fuck from 'round her."

"What the fuck is going on!" I heard Mello in the distance. Lake pulled his gun out and pointed in his direction.

"Ain't shit, my nigga. They just having a friendly conversation." He shrugged.

I started to laugh. "Little bitch finally put out, and the pussy got you throwing ya life away." There was so much venom laced in my voice that my throat shuttered as I said it.

"You should know better than anyone that I don't do well with threats." Heart laughed like he didn't have a care in the world.

"I know you better get that fucking gun off of him," Mello warned from a distance.

"Or what?" Lake asked, chambering a bullet. Security could be seen heading our way. I was caught off guard with this shit. I knew Heart was gonna be pissed, but I wasn't expecting this. That shit was on me for underestimating him; it wouldn't happen again.

"Just stay the fuck away from her." He put the safety back on his gun and placed it back in the back of his pants and turned his back to me, almost like he didn't fear me.

I waited until he took a few steps before I jumped up and took a swing on him that landed in the back of his head. He turned around and started swinging so fucking fast I couldn't keep up. The shit surprised me, and I ended up on my fucking ass again.

"You a bitch ass nigga." Heart stood over me with his fists balled up. I was so fucking mad, if I had my shit, I would blast his ass off his fucking feet. His time was definitely coming. I was gon' let him have this one.

He turned his back again and walked past Mello. When Lake passed, he drew back and knocked the shit out of him. Both them muthafuckas had just signed their death certificates.

Pulling myself up off the floor, I snatched the bottle of Henny out of Mello's hand and turned the bottle up. I was fucking furious.

"Where the fuck were you?" I glared at Mello and looked around for Wynn, who was still nowhere in sight.

"I went to get the fucking bottle like you asked. Seen this sexy as bitch I fuck with from time to time and chopped it up with her." He shrugged like it was no big deal.

"While a nigga was sitting here getting jumped. The fuck you good for!" I fumed. "And where the fuck is Wynn?"

"Last I saw, she was headed outside." He pointed to the door.

"And you let her?" I straightened out my clothes and narrowed my eyes at him. "What the fuck do I need you for?" Just then, Wynn showed her pretty face. She looked at me and then all the mess that was behind me.

"Where the fuck you been?"

"Getting some air, why?" she let roll off of her tongue, something felt off but I let it ride.

I didn't bother to say anything. I just walked out, leaving

them two sitting there looking dumb. I wasn't one to deal with disrespect, especially from someone who wasn't on the same level as me. I needed to put a stop to that shit. Him doing what he did tonight might give other niggas the idea that it was okay. I'd light this fucking city up before I let that happen. Heart was gon' pay for this shit, and that I could promise you.

LAKE

"You ou know we just started a fucking war with that nigga, right?" I said, getting into the car. We were standing outside, waiting to see if he was gon' come out and try some bullshit.

"At this point, I don't even give a fuck. He bleed just like me. Got niggas out here puffing his ass up. He needed to get knocked the fuck down, and I was just the nigga to do that shit." Heart looked from the door and then back at me. "Had you seen Lala's neck, you would feel the same got damn way."

"Shit, I ain't doubting you, my nigga. You know I got you, right or wrong, shit." I dapped him up, and he looked back toward the door just in time to see Mitch head out the door and jump in his car and peel out, leaving Wynn and Mello standing there looking. Mello threw his hands up in the air and hopped in his car, stopping right in from of Wynn, and she hopped right in.

As he rolled out, he looked at me and shook his head. That let me know that I would be seeing him again. He was pussy as fuck because I knew he had his piece in his fucking car. Why in the hell wouldn't he pull out on us?

"Pussy ass nigga," Heart said, seething.

"I was thinking the same thing," I replied, looking down at my phone that was going off like crazy.

"Mira cutting up?" Heart asked, grabbing the handle to his Tahoe.

"Yeah, man. You know how that is. Well, no the fuck you don't, but yo' ass will." I chuckled and he smirked.

It was about got damn time him and Lala stopped all the bull-shit and just fucked and got that shit over with. He loved that girl, and she felt the same way about him. All of that back and forth that they were doing was unnecessary, but that was them.

"Nah, I'd fuck Lala up." We both shared a laugh but for different reasons. Him because he thought that it was my girl that was blowing me up, and he was thinking about going through that shit himself. Me because I knew that it wasn't Mira calling. "You need to answer that shit," he said and nodded to my phone.

I wasn't about to answer the phone right now because Heart would have known that my ass was lying about who had been blowing my shit up all day. Miracle and Wynn were taking turns calling and texting. Hell, if I didn't know any better, I would have thought that they were together or some shit.

Right now, Miracle was texting, talking about we needed to talk, and it was important; said it couldn't wait, and if I didn't hit her back, she was gonna show her ass. I didn't know what the fuck had gotten into her. She used to be so got damn cool. A nigga would go to her crib just to escape the madness. Now she had become the madness.

I didn't have time for her shit today. I had to go home because I got a text from Mira a little while ago letting me know that if I didn't bring my ass home that we were gonna have some problems. I had every intention on taking my ass home right after we finished here. Miracle and Wynn would have to wait.

"We need to figure out what the fuck we gon' do about a connect," Heart said more to himself than me. "I gotta feeling I'ma have to kill that nigga." That came out so fluid that you would never even have thought that he was talking about taking someone's life.

"I might can help with that." I had just found out from Wynn that her father was the one supplying Mitch. If I played my cards right, I might could get the hookup before I cut her ass off.

Her hold on me was that she knew the kind of man her husband was, and if he knew what was going on with us, it would cause problems. Now that Heart had pretty much solidi-fied a war, what the fuck he thought about what we were doing was no longer a concern of mine. Mitch supplied us, and that gave us the means to eat. I was trying to protect that. Now all of that was out the window.

"Wanna fill me in, my nigga." Heart went in his pocket and pulled out his phone and a blunt before he leaned up against his truck.

"Wynn's daddy is his connect."

"And, nigga, that's his wife. The fuck that got to do with anything?"

I looked at him and then dropped my head. I knew I was gon' have to tell him how I knew this information and why I knew for a fact it would work.

"I'm beating that down, and she will pretty much do what the fuck I say if it means getting a piece of the sweet meat." I chuckled, but Heart didn't move or say anything. He just looked ahead like he was trying to process the information.

"Bullshit," he said and finally brought his attention to me. "If I hadn't just fucked shit all up, I would have cussed yo' ass out." We both laughed. We were quiet for a minute before Heart cleared his throat. "I fucked her too." I stretched my eyes and just looked at him.

"The fuck? When?"

"About a year ago, and she tried that 'if you don't fuck me, I'm telling Mitch' bullshit. I told her ass to go ahead; just let me know if she wanted to be buried beside him or not." His face was serious as hell. The nigga didn't have no kind of sense at all. I couldn't help but laugh at his ass.

Ain't this a bitch. All this time I been hiding this shit from this nigga and he was doing the same shit I was. Shit was funny in hindsight. That bitch had some fucking nerve. I was about to turn this whole shit around and get something out of this.

"Hoe ass trick." I shook my head. She wasn't my girl, so I couldn't really be mad. I was just tripping at the fact that she was threatening to blow up my shit.

"She got this apartment that she takes them to and everything."

"That bitch told me that she bought that apartment for me; gave me a key and everything." I went in my pocket and grabbed my keys and dangled them out in front of me.

Heart began to laugh before he held his up. "Yeah, I got that too. Bitch even laced me with a few fits."

"Man, what the fuck!" I smoothed out the shirt that I had on courtesy of Wynn.

"You didn't think you were special, did you? She fucks with all his people. Hell, I know for a fact a few niggas in his camp knocking that pussy down right now." I just looked off. All this fucking time she been had a nigga by the balls and she been spreading pussy like wildfires.

"Say word."

"Muthafucking word!" he said and started laughing. His phone rang, and he looked down at it and got this goofy ass look on his face, and I already knew who it was. Him and Lala were made for each other, and I was happy they found each other.

"Aight, my nigga. You good?" I asked him as I walked to my Camaro that was parked beside his truck.

"Always." He smirked and surveyed the parking lot one more time. "Hook that shit up though."

"Bet. I'll holla at you tomorrow, nigga." I flipped his ass off 'cause his fucking ass was being smart. Shit was crazy, but what did I expect. She was a sneaky bitch, and I knew it. He laughed and jumped in his truck and peeled out.

I had to head home and handle this shit with Mira. I told

Heart that, that was where I'd been lately, and that was the farthest thing from the truth. My time was being stretched thin between her, Miracle, and Wynn. Shit was getting stressful. I had to get a handle on this shit and quick.

Pulling up at the house, all of the lights were on. I knew right then I was about to walk into a fight. I could tell just how pissed she was by the fact that she hadn't called or texted me since she sent that text telling me to bring my ass home.

Putting my key into the door, I slowly opened it. I was met with a hand to the face. She was pissed, but that didn't give her the right to put her hands in my face. Fuck that. I grabbed her by the shoulders and pushed her into the house. I didn't think I pushed her that hard, but when she went flying backward, I knew I had misgauged my strength.

"Muthafucka." She got up and started swinging wildly.

"Yo, Mira, chill the fuck out before you piss me off!"

"Fuck you, Lake. You out here running the fucking streets, not giving a fuck about me and your kids. Laken had a fucking fever so fucking high that he had a seizure, and that was yesterday!" she screamed, making me feel like pure shit. I dropped my head and ran my hands down my face. "Yeah, ya fucking son could've died, muthafucka, and you out here running the fucking streets with God knows who!"

"Mira, I was out here getting this money."

"That's fucking bullshit, and you know it." She swung at me, and I caught her hand.

"Chill now, shit!" I yelled and threw her hand down.

"You told me shit was gonna get better, and it ain't better, Lake. I'm done."

"You're not done."

"Wanna bet?" She tried to walk past me, but I grabbed her arm, and she jerked away. The look in her eyes scared me because I had never seen it before. I knew I fucked up, but she couldn't be done wit' a nigga. I couldn't have that.

"Look, shit been hectic, but it ain't what you think, Mira," I lied. "Now where's my son?"

"He's not here, just like I'm about to not be." She tried to walk past me again, and I grabbed her at the same time my phone went off. She looked me in the eye, daring me to answer it. I didn't have a choice though. After what happened tonight, I needed to be on my shit. I released her arm and went for my phone, but I stepped in front of her so that she couldn't get past me.

"This is what I'm talking about." Her hands found her hip, and she started tapping her foot on the floor. I could tell that she was about to cry because she was chewing on her lip. I hated to see her cry, especially when I was the cause of it.

I knew I hadn't been the best man to her, but a nigga was just caught up in this shit with Wynn. That and the fact that I was addicted to pussy, had my relationship on the brinks of destruction.

"Chill." I looked down at my phone and looked at the text from Wynn.

Wynn: I need to see you now!!!

I chose to ignore it. The days of her running shit with me

were over. I was gonna be dictating what the fuck went on from this point on. Depending on her connection with her father would determine if I fucked with her or not.

"I'm tired, Lake." The desperation in her voice alarmed me. Had a nigga second guessing in that moment if I was really good for her. Maybe I should let her go. She deserved better than what I was trying to give at the moment. Nah, I couldn't do that shit. I loved her too much to see her walk out the door. She was just gon' have to be patient with a nigga. My phone went off again.

Wynn: Mitch!

That was all the text said, causing me to bite down on my back teeth and grind them. The shit that happened tonight put some shit into play, and Wynn might have known what that is. On the other hand, it could have very well been a setup, but Wynn was feeling a nigga too much to set me up. Right?

I looked up at Mira, the love that was normally housed in her eyes was fading and her emotionless stare scared me but I needed to go check this out, my life was depending on it. At least that's what I was telling myself to keep from feeling like shit for wanting to escape her wrath in this moment.

"Go!" She laughed.

"Look, we will talk about this when I get back. I promise we gon' work this shit out." I grabbed at her, but she moved out of my grasp and turned to walk upstairs. "I love you, Mira."

That 'I love you' wasn't returned, but I didn't expect it to be. I knew how she felt about me. I also knew what I was doing to her was tearing her down. I needed to get my shit in order before she really left my black ass.

Once Mira disappeared up the stairs, I headed out the door, locking it. I hopped in my car and headed in the direction of Wynn's little fuck pad she had for us and God knows who else. My phone had been on one today. I looked down at it, and it was Miracle again. This time I decided to answer the phone because it didn't look like she was backing down anytime soon.

"What!" I yelled.

"Don't fucking talk to me like that, Lake. I'm not her. I need to talk to you about something that's important."

"Talk!"

"I'm not about to tell you this over the phone. You need to get here and now," she demanded.

"Nah, I can't do that."

"What do you mean you can't do that, Lake? I need to see you."

"Say what you got to say before I hang the fuck up." I was getting close to my destination, and this back and forth was starting to get on my nerves. I didn't know who these women thought they were, but evidently, I had given them the notation that they had say so over what the fuck I did.

"I'm pregnant, Lake." That shit sucked the wind right out of me. How in the fuck was she pregnant? How was I so fucking careless? I couldn't have been that fucking careless, or could I? Fuck!

"I ain't got time for this shit right now." I hit the steering wheel. "What the fuck!"

"Yeah, well I ain't got shit to do with that. It happened, and we're having a baby," she said with more attitude than I was willing to deal with at the present moment. Instead of answering her, I just hung up the phone and threw it in the seat next to me.

What the fuck was I gonna do? Miracle wasn't just gonna get an abortion. She wasn't that type of chick. That was one of the things that I loved about her. She was so head strong and didn't take shit from no one. Her cool personality drew me in. I guess this explained why she'd been so fucking clingy and needy.

How was I gonna explain this shit to Mira? There was no way that I would be able to hide this shit for too long. Especially not with the both of them being attached to Lala. Fuck! I pulled up to Wynn's and knew I had to make this quick. I needed to get back to make sure that Mira was good and then I needed to have a face to face with Miracle.

I grabbed my phone and sent a text that said come outside. She tried to argue, but I told her that if she didn't come, I would leave. Minutes later, she came strutting out of the building and hopped her sexy ass in my car.

"Why can't you come in?" she said with a pout. I wanted to slap the shit off her face with her hoe ass.

"'Cause I can't stay." I looked at her, and she rolled her eyes. "Man, what's up?"

"The way I see it, I got information that you need, and I want something out of it." She smirked.

"Get out, man. I ain't got time for this shit." I grabbed my keys that were still in the ignition and prepared to crank my car up again. "From what I hear, you should be good in the dick department."

"I don't know what the hell you're talking about. Outside of my husband, you're the only one I'm fucking." The lie poured from her mouth so effortlessly, I didn't bother to correct her because the way I saw it, I was about to use this little shit between us to my advantage. So I just nodded and smirked. "Lake, you want to know this. Trust me." She bit her lips as her eyes left mine and traveled down to my lap.

I already knew she was gon' be on that bullshit when I came over to this bitch. That was just who she was. I hated that I ever started to fuck with her, but here we were. Hell, I was stressed as fuck and could use a stress reliever, so I unbuckled my pants, slid them down, and pushed the seat back as far as it would go. Hell, if she was giving away the pussy for free, I may as well get my share.

I looked over, and she flashed a sexy smirk. Hiking up her dress, she was about to climb over the seat, and I stopped her. I reached in the glove compartment and grabbed a condom. After that shit Miracle just called me with, a nigga was being fucking careful. Once I had the condom securely on, I nodded for her to come sit on it.

I knew I probably shouldn't have been doing this, but a nigga wasn't one to turn down pussy. That was why my ass was in the predicament that I was in now.

"Ssssssss," she said as she straddled my lap and my head penetrated her opening. "Ummm, fuck." Wynn's pussy was A1, and she knew just what to do with it. That was one of the reasons I let her get away with that threatening shit. As bad as I wanted to put that shit on not wanting her to say shit to Mitch, a lot of it was because I loved the way she felt. "Damn." She had finally sucked all of me in and had started to move nice and slow. She threw her head back, but I stopped her. "What the fuck, Lake!"

"Why did you text me?" I looked her in the eyes. She was in a vulnerable spot, and that was a sure way to get the information that I needed.

"After I cum." She tried to move under my hold, but I grabbed her tighter. She sighed and slumped her shoulders in a defeated way. "He said that you and Heart disrespected him, and he had to teach you a lesson. He didn't say when or where, but he's coming after you." If she wasn't soaking my dick, I would throw her the fuck off me. I already knew that shit; I thought she had specifics.

"That's it?" I mugged her.

"Yeah. What the fuck y'all do to piss him off? I don't think I ever seen him like that."

"He tried to get at Lala, Heart's girl, and when she turned his bitch ass down, he tried to rape her," I said not even realizing it. "That's all he said?"

"Yeah." She shrugged. "Who the fuck is Lala?" She snarled her nose up.

"Don't fucking worry about it. I'm telling you now, fucking with her can be bad for your health." My eyes bore into hers so that she knew I wasn't bullshitting.

Lala didn't want shit to do with Mitch. That was his perverted ass after her, but that was how Wynn operated. She didn't care who was after who; all she heard was someone was trying to cash in on her good fortune, regardless of the situation. Just the thought that Mitch might be interested in someone else pissed her off, even though she was currently riding my dick, and according to Heart, everybody in Mooresville, NC.

She folded her arms across her chest and sat there and pouted like I gave a fuck. For a while, we sat there, me still inside her just having a fucking stare down. I was ready to get the fuck away from her. I grabbed her hips and tried to lift her until she started to move slowly in my lap again. Fuck. She got me every time.

"Damn," I said, looking down at the way she was rolling her hips in my lap. That was how it went with us. I couldn't stand her ass, and she was pissed that she couldn't control me like she wanted to, but we connected through some hard-core fucking.

Leaning down, she tried to kiss me, but I turned my head. She knew I didn't play that shit. Only people touched these lips were Mira and Miracle, that was it. I actually cared about them. I could put a bullet in Wynn's head, and the only thing I would miss would be the pussy.

Placing her hands on my chest for leverage, she started bouncing lightly. Shit was feeling good as fuck. Made the trip worth it because she damn sure didn't tell me shit.

"I need you to... ahhhh, fuck, Wynn." I bit my lip and started matching her stroke for stroke from the bottom. "Shit, ride that shit." She had sped up, and I could tell that she was almost at her peek because her mouth hung open. "I need to talk to your father, fuck!" I grabbed her hips and pounded into her from the bottom. I was about to blow my load when all of a sudden, my door flew open and Wynn was being pulled off me. "What the fuck?"

My first thought was that it was Mitch, so I reached for my

gun and aimed it at whoever it was, but to my surprise, it was Mira. She was dragging Wynn through the grass by her hair. I tried to separate them, but she kicked me in my nuts that were exposed because I hadn't had time to get myself situated.

I surveyed the parking lot, trying to figure out how she got here and where her car was. My attention was drawn to Mira screaming. Wynn had picked up a brick and hit her across the head with it. I rushed over and pushed Wynn down when she raised her hand again.

"What the fuck!" she yelled out.

"I knew you were up to no good," Mira cried out.

"No, baby, it's not like that." I tried to lie, but there wasn't much I could say, and when Mira passed out in my arms, I started to hate myself. "Mira, wake up, baby! Wake up!"

What the fuck had I done? I picked her up bridal style and threw her in the passenger side of my car and rushed to Lake Norman Regional. She had to be okay. I would never be able to forgive myself if she wasn't okay. I said a quick prayer to the man upstairs as I wove in and out of traffic trying to get to the hospital.

LALA

*A*fter Heart came back last night, he explained to me what happened at the club. I asked him not to do that because I didn't want to cause problems with him and Mitch. I just wanted the muthafucka to stay the fuck away from me. I just hated that Heart had to step in like that, but I should've known he would.

"What you thinking about?" Heart asked as he kissed my exposed shoulder. We were laying on the couch with my back to his chest, watching ratchet TV.

"Us," I said softly. This was everything that I always wanted. I knew that we could make it work, but I had this nagging feeling in the back of my mind that something was gonna go wrong. I was trying to get it out of my head, but it was there, and I couldn't deny the feeling that it was giving me.

"What about us?" He pressed his semi-hard dick against my

ass. We were currently naked from the night before. Heart said he wanted to feel my skin, and I wasn't complaining because it felt good to be that close to him.

"I want this to work."

"Me too." His tone was unsure, which caused me to look over my shoulder at him.

"You don't think we can?"

"I do. I just know it's gon' be hard as fuck. I love you, you know that, but I also know that I'm not good for you. My life ain't good for you. I want you to succeed, and I would hate myself if I prevented you from doing that." He got silent for a minute. "Don't you understand where I'm coming from?"

His explanation was all over the place, but I got what he was saying. He was always looking out for me, so this was no different. Only thing was he was trying to protect me from the one thing that I longed for: him.

"I get that, Heart, but this is what I want. If you want to see me happy and you want to see me succeed, then you'll be this for me." I folded into him and he accepted me. "This is what I need to be all of those things you just said," I whispered.

He responded by lifting my leg and sliding into me from the side. I gasped because I was still getting used to his size. When his hand found my nipple, I was in heaven. It was like our bodies were so in sync, this just made sense to me.

"Shit," he moaned in my ear as he delivered slow, purposeful strokes, taking my body to new heights. "I love this shit."

"Ummm, I love it too," I said as his hand traveled down my

body and found my button. Putting the right amount of pressure to it and causing me to lift my leg so I could feel more of him.

Every stroke he delivered told me how he was feeling in this moment. I felt like I was having an outer body experience, like I had no control over my body and what it was doing. Grabbing my stomach, he slightly rolled me over while he was still inside of me, placing one foot on the ground and lifting my ass so that it was tooted up for him just the way he preferred it.

"Just like that." He slapped my ass and then grabbed two handfuls and went to work. "Shit."

He slowed down just a bit so that he could paint some love on my g-spot. I could literally feel this man in my stomach, and it was the best feeling in the world at the moment.

"You're gonna make me cum," I said the minute he grabbed my ponytail and pulled it enough to take the holder off. My hair fell around my face as he grabbed a handful and forced my head back, and that was it. I came all over his dick.

"Fuck!" he growled as he released his load into my unprotected womb. I needed to go and get on somebody's birth control before I ended up someone's mother. "Damn, you got some good pussy."

"Ummm, well thank you." I panted as he slid out of me. "Lord Jesus," I said as I collapsed on the couch. I was spent, and he thought that was funny.

"Damn, it's like that?"

"Hell yeah, shit!" I buried my head in the pillow. I could hear him moving around me but I was too focused on drifting off to sleep to care about what he was doing.

"Fuck!" he yelled out and threw his phone on the table, and that caused me to look up at him.

I gave him a questioning look. I could tell that he was trying to calm himself down before he filled me in on what was going on, but it was failing miserably. I could see the worry lines on his handsome face. "Mira in the hospital."

"What! Why? What the fuck happened?"

"Some shit went down. Get up; let's go. We need to get to the hospital."

Not bothering to ask anything else, I jumped up and headed to the back to wash up and get dressed so that we could go and check on her. I swear if she got caught up in Lake's bullshit, I was fucking him up on sight.

I hit the sink and took a quick hoe bath and brushed my teeth. I had to make sure my girl was okay; a shower would have to wait. Heart joined me in the bathroom. He was seemingly upset; mentally, he wasn't even present anymore. His mind was clearly somewhere else. I didn't want to stress him out any more than he appeared to be, but I needed to know the answer to the question I was about to ask.

"Does this have anything to do with what happened last night?"

"Nah, and that's the fucked up part about it," he said and shook his head. He walked out of the bathroom before I could ask him what that meant. In a world of his own, he moved around my tiny apartment, getting his things together. "You ready?" He finally asked after snapping out of his thoughts.

"Yes," was all I said, and he looked at me. I had seen him

like this before, and I knew when he was pissed, he got quiet and calm. It was always best to let him be when he was like this. "I'm sorry." He walked to me and pressed his lips against mine. "You gotta be patient with a nigga; this is new to me."

"But I'm not new to you, so you don't have to apologize. I know how yo' crazy ass is." I shook my head, and he laughed.

"True." He kissed me again and headed out the door with me right behind him.

The ride to the hospital was a quiet one. We were both in our own thoughts. I just hoped like hell that Mira was okay. Heart didn't reveal any information about what happened other than the fact that she was in the hospital. I had no idea what the extent was or anything like that.

When we got to the hospital, Heart grabbed my hand as we walked through the doors, like he was protecting me from something. I didn't know what that was until he opened the doors and I came face to face with my mother.

I had mixed emotions because, on one hand, I missed her, and then I remembered the shit that she had put me through since my dad died, and all of that went out the window. I hadn't seen her since the night of the fight. I made it my business to stay the fuck away from the bottom of the Creek, and she didn't know where I stayed; at least to my knowledge she didn't.

"Laurence, you look so good, baby. How are you?" She stepped up like she was gonna hug me, but I put my hand up to stop her, and she dropped her head.

I took a good look at her, and if I didn't know any better, I would say that she was getting better. She looked to have put on some weight. Her normally dull skin had a slight glow to it. It had only been a few months since I'd seen her last.

"Are you clean, Mom?" I asked, and she looked up at me and smiled. I saw the sparkle in her eye that she used to have when my dad was alive; that sparkle that I missed so much. Tears stung my eyes as I flung my arms around her neck. "I'm so happy that you're clean, Mom. God I've missed you.

Just that fast, all the hate I had in my heart for her disappeared. All I had ever wanted was to see my mother bounce back from the tragedy that damn near killed her. I knew she loved Dad; I just never knew she loved him more than she loved me.

"Laurence!" I heard someone calling from behind me. "You look just like your father."

"Darren?" I questioned. Darren was my dad's best friend and right-hand man when he was in the streets. When my dad died, he left town because it was too much for him to deal with. He said that he couldn't do this without my dad. So he picked up and left. What was he doing here?

"In the flesh." He smiled and came and joined the hug with me and my mom like we were some kind of family or something. I wasn't feeling this at all, so I removed myself from the group hug and took my place beside Heart, who wrapped me in his arms.

"You look so happy, baby." My mom reached out and moved my hair behind my ear. "You always did have the biggest crush on him." She smiled. I wanted to say how the hell do you know when you spent the majority of the time shoving liquor down your throat.

"Yeah, you look happy too." My tone was suggestive, and she clearly caught on.

"Darren came back to town a couple months ago, and he came to find me to see how I was. I was in bad shape, and he helped me get to where I am right now."

"So it took a man for you to get your shit together?" I was hurt and pissed all at the same time. Don't get me wrong, I was happy that she was sober, but the fact that she couldn't do that shit for me, hurt. It took a man to come into her life for her to realize she needed help? What kind of shit was that? "I wasn't good enough for you to want to change your life? For five years straight, you treated me like I was a stranger on the street, and now he pops up and you're ready to get help. What kind of sense does that make, Mama?" I didn't realize I was crying until the tears kissed my cheeks. Heart wrapped me up in his arms.

"Let's go," he whispered in my ear, and I nodded. I couldn't take this right now.

"Can't you just be happy for me, child? I was broken when your dad left us," she tried to explain.

"He fucking died!" I yelled louder than I intended. "He didn't leave; he died."

"Well you know what I mean; I just couldn't handle it. I was sick and I apologize for that. I don't know what else to say." She shrugged, like the things she put me through didn't matter.

"Don't say anything." I smiled through my tears and took off down the hall with Heart in tow.

All you could hear down the hallway were our footsteps and

my sniffles. Heart grabbed me right before we got to the intensive care unit. He encased me in his arms and just let me cry.

"Why am I not good enough for her?" I cried more to myself than to him, but he didn't hesitate to answer the question.

"Some people look for love and validation in places that it doesn't exist. It's not that you're not good enough, it's just you couldn't give her what she thought she needed to get better. Your mom loves you; don't doubt that. She's just addicted to companionship just as much as she was addicted to the alcohol. There is nothing that you could have done different to change that. It's just who she is. It's up to you to accept that, and if you can't, then love her from a distance."

The words he spoke resonated through my soul, and he was right. What my mother felt she needed, I couldn't provide, so until she got that, she would never get better. Seems like she found that. I still didn't know how I felt about it, so until I did, I was gonna keep my distance.

"Thank you." I smiled through my tears and leaned up and kissed his lips. "That's why I've always loved you."

He smiled and grabbed my hand, and we headed to the room that Lake told us that Mira was in. This man was my soulmate, and I knew it.

MIRA

I pretended like I was still out while I listed to Lake profess his love for me and how sorry he was. I wasn't buying into that shit though. He had made a fool of me, and I was not about to sit back and take it. I knew he was cheating on me; I just had this nagging feeling in the pit of my gut that he was up to no good.

From the day I saw him come out of that apartment complex talking about he was doing business, I'd had my eye on him. I would show up to the apartment complex on days that he didn't come home and see his car there. I would have gotten out to see where the hell he was, but I had my kids with me.

That was what brought me to my breaking point. When I got to the point where I was taking my kids with me all time of night to look for him, I knew that my time was up with this situation. I was never one to chase a man, and the fact that I was out here doing that woke something up in me. When he left the house tonight to go "check on something," I knew this was my chance to catch him.

I let him go before I left because I already knew where he was going; he spent most of his time there. Hell, for a minute, he had me thinking that it was where he did his business as much as he was there, but something was telling me different, and I was glad I stuck with that. Otherwise, I would have missed out on my opportunity to catch him in his dirt.

"Aye, bruh," I heard Lake say when the door opened and shut. I wanted to see who it was, but I didn't want him to know I was up because I didn't have shit to say to him right now. "Lala, you good?" he asked.

"What happened to Mira?" she asked, ignoring his question. *My girl.*

"Let me holla at you." Heart sounded like he was pissed off, so I wondered if he knew about him knocking that bitch down. "We'll be back." I could hear him kissing her, and I was happy for them.

The last time I talked to her, she was telling me that they decided to get together and make it work finally. After all that cat and mouse shit that they were doing, it was about time. She loved him, and I knew that he loved her; they were good for each other.

When the door shut, I opened my eyes in search for Lala. She was standing by the window, staring out. I could see the tears rolling down her cheek, and I wondered what was going on. There was a defeated aura around her, and that wasn't like her.

She had been through a lot in her young years, and she always kept a positive attitude no matter what.

"Aww, sis, don't cry. I'm good," I joked in a hushed tone. My head was banging, and talking any louder would have caused me more pain than I wanted to deal with.

"Oh shit, you're up?" She smiled and moved toward the bed. "What the hell happened? Heart won't tell me shit." She frowned.

It was my turn to shed a few tears. Shit was all fucked up, and I didn't know where to start. I didn't know how life got all fucked up for us and how we went from being so in love to me out here fighting a bitch that I caught riding his dick.

"Don't cry." She bent down and hugged me. "It's gonna be okay."

"No it won't." I cried harder. "I'm leaving Lake." She leaned back and looked me in my eyes to see if I was serious. My eyes didn't waver, and neither did my words. I was done with him, and there was nothing that anyone could say to change my mind.

The fact that he was out fucking a bitch while my son was in the hospital having a fucking seizure let me know that he was not the man for me. I needed someone that was gonna be here and be loyal, and Lake did neither.

"What happened?"

"So, Lake been doing some shady shit lately. He ain't been coming home, and when he does, it's to shower then sleep and then gone again the next morning before I even wake up." I took a deep breath to try and control my emotions. "I followed him, and he had been going to see this bitch.

"Bullshit?" I nodded my head to let her know that what I was saying was real.

"That ain't even the fucked-up part."

"That muthafucka," she said through pierced lips.

"Laken had a fever so high that I had to take him to the hospital where he had a seizure." She covered her mouth and gasped. "Yeah, and I couldn't get a hold of Lake for shit. Rode by the apartments that I had seen him come from, and there he was. So I went home and texted him and told his ass that if he didn't come home, me and the kids wouldn't be there, and still no Lake."

"Girl."

"You just don't know." I shook my head. "So I dropped my kids off with my mama, and I waited on that nigga to come home. When he did, we argued, and then all of a sudden, he had to leave. I let him leave, and then I jumped in my car and went right to the apartments that I had seen him in numerous times, and again, there he was."

"What the fuck is wrong with him?" Lala was pissed.

"I parked my car around the corner and walked to the complex. I walked to the building that his car was parked in front of, and I had every intention of knocking on every fucking door until I found his ass." I got choked up just thinking about seeing her pleasing him in a way that only I was supposed to. "Before I could even reach the stairs, something told me to look back at his car. It was dark, but I could clearly see that someone was in the car." I wiped the tears that had fallen with the back of my hand. "I took a better look, and all I saw was ass."

"Ass? The fuck?"

"Some bitch was riding him in the front seat of his car; the front seat that I've been in. There is no telling how many times he's had her in that car."

"Oh shit."

"I yanked that door open and pulled her ass out of that fucking car and whooped her fucking ass all over that parking lot. The bitch got loose from my grasp somehow and picked up a brick and hit me in the head with it. I don't remember shit else, 'cause I blacked out and woke up here."

Once I was done, I really broke down. As tough as I liked to act, I really loved Lake. I never thought in a million years that I would be sitting here trying to decide if I was moving or if I was setting his shit outside of the house that we shared.

Lala hugged me, and I cried on her shoulder. I didn't even lift my head when I heard the door open. I was sure that it was Heart and Lake, because I heard Heart say "shit" when he walked in.

"You ain't shit, you know that?" Lala said with so much venom in her voice.

"I know, sis. I'ma make that shit right, I promise. I will do whatever it is that I have to do to make sure that she knows that shit will never happen again," he said like he had a choice in our future.

I didn't bother saying anything. I just kept my head buried in Lala's shoulder while she went back and forth with him. I heard my phone go off to the left of me, so I leaned over to grab it. I hit the fingerprint button to open it, and what I saw hurt me more than what I had just went through.

I pushed Lala away from me and looked at the picture of the pregnancy test that appeared in the messages. That's when I noticed that Lake picked up the wrong phone when he left. He grabbed mine and left his. I had my fingerprint stored in his phone and his was stored in mine.

The last time he started doing his disappearing acts, I made him do that shit so I would have access to it, and I guess he forgot about it when he started doing his dirt, because here we were. The tears started to flow freely this time.

"Mira, what's wrong?" Lala asked and then snatched the phone from me. She looked at it and then she got this weird ass look on her face. "The fuck Miracle texting you pictures of a pregnancy test for?" she asked and then looked at me.

"That's a question you should be asking Lake, seeing as though that's his fucking phone." The number wasn't stored, but Lala just revealed who it was. I automatically thought that it was the bitch I fucked up today, but it looks like my man was for everybody. "Wait, your friend Miracle?" It hit me who she said, and that sent alarms up everywhere.

"What the fuck!" Lake said and headed to the bed.

I was gon' throw the phone at his fucking head, but I didn't even have the energy to do that. I shoved it in his chest the minute he was close enough. He looked at the phone and then at me. My body was filled with so much hatred for this man right now. I didn't think I'd ever felt like this about anybody.

"Man, what the fuck," Heart said from the corner. His hands moved down his face in a frustrated way. He looked at me and then at Lala, who had a nasty look on her face.

"You knew about this?" she asked him.

"Nah, you ain't about to do that shit. That ain't got nothing to do with us. That's their business."

He shut her down, but I didn't doubt for a second that he knew. They were boys, so his loyalty was with Lake, not me. My concern was whose loyalty was Lala's with.

"You gon' tell me that you didn't?" My tone was harsh.

"Are you insinuating that I did?" She was defensive. I just didn't know if it was because she was offended that I would think she would do something like that or if it was because she was guilty.

"As much as you're with her, you not about to tell me that you didn't know that they were fucking."

"Miracle is my best friend, yes, but we do not spend every waking minute together, and you know that better than anyone. I work, and I'm in school, and so is she, so no, I didn't know, and how dare you insinuate that I did." She stood up and put her hands on her hips. "I told Miracle to stay away from Lake years ago when she hinted around the fact that she was attracted to him. I told her that you were good people and he would never leave you so she would be wasting her time. I would never do you like that, and you should know that. I ain't like that, Mira." Her watery eyes were playing at my heartstrings, but right now, I didn't know who I could trust.

"I want all of you out of here," I said, wiping my eyes.

"I'm not going nowhere," Lake said like he had a choice in the matter. He had his phone in his hands, so I was sure that he was texting that bitch. I couldn't wait to see her.

"Wanna fucking bet, you disrespectful muthafucka?"

"Mira, that ain't my baby." I could see through the lie as it left his lips; he was worried, and I could tell.

"So why you standing there looking like you could shit yourself any minute, Lake? I know you."

"Baby, I swear it ain't what you think."

"Then how the fuck is it!" I screamed to the top of my lungs. My head was pounding. "Just get out! Get out! Get out! Get out!"

I kept yelling until the nurse and security came in there and escorted all of them out of my room. I was broken. I didn't know where to go from here. How could my whole life fall apart like this in one day? I balled up on the little bed and cried until I couldn't cry anymore. It was then that I made a promise to myself that I would never in my life let a man make a fool of me again.

I was going home and getting rid of all his shit and changing my locks. I was done, and I was about to show him just how much I was. I didn't deserve any of this. I was a good woman and mother. Karma was a bitch, and I hoped she ruined his ass.

MIRACLE

*L*ake had me fucked up. I didn't know what the fuck had
gotten into him as of lately, but he told me that he
wanted to be with me. He made a promise to me, and
now he was treating me like I was one of his whores. I was not
about to sit around and allow that shit to happen. He was gon'
have to step up and take care of this baby. I didn't make it by
myself, and I wasn't about to raise it by myself either.

He was as much to blame as I was with this. No, I didn't tell
him that I was off my birth control, but he wasn't doing anything
to prevent a pregnancy either. He stayed blessing me with his
seeds every chance he got.

I had been calling Lake and texting him back to back, and he
hadn't answered me not once. I never thought that I would have
to go through this with him. I just thought that he would embrace
this moment. He told me he loved me and he wanted to be with

me; I thought this baby would solidify that. He was proving me wrong by the second.

I needed to talk to someone, but the only friend I really had was Lala, and I knew that she wouldn't understand. I could almost guarantee that she would be pissed with me; one, for lying to her about it, and two, for doing it after she begged me not to. She was gonna find out sooner or later though, and I'd rather I be the one to tell her.

Fall was starting to settle in, and the weather was beautiful. The sun kissed my cheeks providing the perfect amount of warmth. It wasn't cold, nor was it hot; just perfect for the conversation I was about to have. This was not about to be easy. I just hoped that Lala would understand where I was coming from.

"Aye, girl, look at all that ass," I said, trying to ease the situation that was about to happen.

She was so lost in her thoughts that she didn't even see me coming, but when she finally noticed me, the look on her face was not a pleasant one. I stopped in my tracks and debated on whether or not to go to her with this today. I knew Lala, and if she was in a bad mood, she was gon' take everything I said the wrong way.

"How could you?" she finally said after a few minutes of a stare down.

"How could I what? What you talking about, Lala?"

"Now is not the time, Lala," Heart said in a warning tone. He tried to pull her away from me, but I was now curious as to what she was so pissed about. "Let's go, La." He tried one last attempt to get her to let whatever conversation he didn't want her to have with me, go.

"You just had to go after him, huh, after I told you not to. Why did you have to do that, Miracle? I told you that man had a fucking family!" she yelled.

I swallowed hard, trying to get my thoughts together. The one thing that I didn't want was for her to find out this shit before I had a chance to tell her. I knew that Lala was friends with Mira, but she was my best friend, so I expected her to understand what the fuck I was going through. I mean, you can't help who you loved, and she of all people should understand that.

"I was gonna tell you."

"That's fucking funny, because I just ask you about that shit in the mall, and you looked me right in the face and fucking lied." She was pissed off, and I could tell by the red hues that were taking over her normal honey colored skin.

"Can we just talk about this?" I asked, and she smacked her lips and rolled her eyes. "I know this puts you in a bad spot because you're friends with the both of us, but to be honest, this really has nothing to do with you, La." I tried to be nice and calm about it, but truth be told, it wasn't her business. The only reason I was even gon' tell her was because it was gonna come out about the baby, and I wanted her to hear the shit from me. She was my best friend, and I was carrying her godchild. "I mean, I know I was wrong for not telling you the truth about me and Lake, but I couldn't help who I fell in love with."

"Ha! In love with?" She threw her head back and laughed, and I could already tell that this conversation was about to take a turn for the worse. The smart thing would have been to walk away, but I couldn't; my pride wouldn't let me. "Girl, you are delusional. I don't know what that man been feeding you, but it's a bunch of bullshit. He's never gonna leave Mira and his kids. Where do you think he is now? With her, at the hospital, making sure she's okay!" she yelled at me.

"You don't know what you're talking about. He's only with her for the kids. He doesn't love her; he loves me. As soon as the kids are old enough to understand, he's gon' leave and be with me."

"Is that what he told you? And you believed that bullshit? From the outside looking in, I can tell you that he just played you for a got damn fool, and you fell for it." Disappointment was written all over her face, and it was making me feel some kind of way, but I would never let her know that. "He denied you, honey. He told Mira that it wasn't his baby."

"You're lying!"

That hit hard, and I wanted to break down right then and there. Ever since I told Lake about me being pregnant, he'd been ignoring me and dodging my calls. I took it as him trying to figure out a way to tell Mira, but now I wasn't so sure.

"Did he tell you what happened today?" She narrowed her eyes at me.

"La, that's enough." Heart stepped in again.

"No, she needs to hear this." She snapped her neck at him, and he threw his hands up in surrender. "The only reason Mira is in the hospital was because she ran up on Lake's ass fucking another bitch, and when she caught his lying ass, she beat the bitch's ass. Not being able to take a L, the weak bitch hit her in the head with a brick." I felt like my heart balled up and punch me in the chest, and I guess it showed on my face, and it caused Lala to keep going. "You sitting out here pregnant with that nigga's baby, and he out here slanging dick like he getting paid for the shit."

I had never seen Lala so judgmental in my life. I didn't know what was going on with her, but I wasn't feeling it. The whole five years we'd been friends, we had never had a fight like the one we were having at this present moment. It was like I didn't even know her ass.

"Sounds like to me you riding for that bitch more than you riding for me."

"You're dumber than I thought, Miracle." She chuckled angrily. "It's not about who riding for who. It's about right and wrong, and you dead wrong right now."

"Why, because I fell in love with a man who happened to be in a relationship? I couldn't help it, Lala. You should know better than anybody you can't help who you love." The tears involuntarily started to fall, and I didn't stop them.

Hurt was an understatement. Not only was my man out here fucking other bitches besides the one I knew about, he was also out here denying me and this baby. I needed to talk to Lake and fast because he had some fucking explaining to do.

"You fell in love with another woman's man; that is completely different from what I got going on, boo." Her head was held high like she was somehow better than me, and that pissed me off. "The bad part about the whole thing is I told you not to fuck with him because this is what would happen, but you didn't listen. So, this is your fault."

"Fuck you, La. Like I said, this ain't got nothing to do with you and—"

"It had something to do with me when you got people thinking I'm fraud because I'm friends with you," she pointed out.

"Well you ain't got to fucking worry about that no more," I said and then turned around and headed back toward my apartment at the bottom of the Creek.

"Good!" I heard her yell behind me and then Heart fussing at her for acting on her emotions.

I didn't even care if she was acting on emotions. I didn't think our friendship would ever be the same again. The way she just threw me to the wayside for something that had nothing to do with her showed me just how strong our friendship was. She never even asked about the baby. The way she talked, it seemed as though she thought the baby was a mistake, and that hurt the most.

When I got to my apartment, I threw myself on the bed and bawled my eyes out. I cried until I couldn't produce another sound or tear. How did things go south so fast? I would never know, but I needed Lake here with me to help me through this and give me the answers that I needed.

I picked up the phone and called him, but it went straight to voicemail. I tried numerous times after that and got the same result. I curled up in a little ball, finding the tears I thought were gone, I cried myself to sleep.

MITCH

*T*he Creek been quiet lately. I had my eyes over there, and wasn't shit moving. Heart and Lake came and went, but nothing major. I didn't know where the fuck they'd been getting their work from and where the fuck they'd been selling it, because I hadn't heard shit from them since that night at the club.

I wanted them muthafuckas to think that things had settled, and it was all good, like I forgot about what happened. That was when I planned to hit them, and hard. I didn't know who the fuck they thought I was, but I wasn't one to fuck around with. Letting niggas punk you like that in public opened the doors for other muthafuckas to think that shit was okay. I had a few try me in the past week, and I had to put them in they place.

Heart and Lake were two of my most loyal workers, and I hated to have to get rid of them, but they brought this on themselves. I heard the door open, and I turned to see who the fuck it was. I was chilling in the living room at the crib, so I had to wait for the person to walk through the foyer.

"The fuck happened to your face?" I asked Wynn the minute she came into my view. I hadn't seen her in a few days. I had been so wrapped up in trying to get shit straight and in place before I had to take out Heart and Lake that I didn't even realize until now. "And where the fuck have you been?"

"Oh, now you worried about where I been? You wasn't worried about me when you were out here trying to rape little ass girls, now. were you?" She rolled her eyes and walked past me and up the stairs.

What the fuck did she just say? How in the hell did she know about that? Who would have said something about that unless it was Heart or Lake, but why in the hell would she have crossed their paths? I got up and took off up the stairs with her. When I opened the room door, she was sitting on the bed with her head in her hands.

"What the fuck are you talking about, Wynn?"

"Who the fuck is Lala, and why do you want her so much that you are willing to try and rape her to get it? Is that what you have resulted to?"

"Ain't nobody raping nobody. Do I look like the nigga that needs to rape some got damn body? Be for real." I patted my chest. I didn't technically try and rape her; all I wanted to do was get what I was owed.

"So who is she?"

"This little bitch running around chasing after me. She was

walking home, and I offered her a ride, and when she tried to get at me and I turned her young ass down, she cried rape. The little hoe is only nineteen years old. The fuck I'ma do with her?" I lied.

Lord knew if I had the chance, I would knock her sexy ass down with the quickness, but fuck her. She done caused enough fucking trouble in my life, and I was about to start some in hers. Starting with getting rid of her little boyfriend.

"Maybe I need to pay the little bitch a visit," she said, checking out her nails.

"Do what you feel, baby." I shrugged. "Now what the fuck happened to your face, and where the fuck have you been?"

Wynn was a complicated character, and you had to handle her a certain way. If she had something in her mind, she was gone feed off that shit until she got the answers that she wanted, and she didn't give a fuck what else was going on.

"I've been at my mother's house," she said nonchalantly. It sounded like a lie, but I let it go for now.

"And your face?"

She dropped her head, and the waterworks started. I gave her a minute to get all of the theatrics out so that I could get the story of what happened to her face. I knew my wife, and she had to put on a show in order to get her point across, so I gave her the audience that she desired.

"Lake did it," she said through her sobs.

"Who?" I said just to be clear that I heard her correctly. There was no way that nigga was bold enough to put his hands on my wife. They had balls—I'd give them that—but the muthafuckas weren't crazy. I knew about his girl, and his kids and I would hate to involve innocent bystanders. "Wynn, who the fuck did you say?"

"Lake. He followed me and then asked me to connect him with my father because he knows that's who your connect is." She sniffed. "When I told him no, he went crazy. I had never seen him like that."

"What you mean?"

"Huh?" She sniffed and looked at me.

"You said you had never seen him like that before. What do you mean? You ain't around that nigga like that to be able to say what he is and ain't like." I ran my hand across my head. The tears dried up real quick, and she just stared at me like a deer caught in headlights. "Wynn."

"No, I was just saying the times that I was around him with you, you know partying and stuff." She shrugged. Her nervous demeanor put a bad taste in my mouth.

"You sure?"

"Yeah, baby. What else would I mean?" She was starting to get defensive. "I just told you that nigga put his hands on me, and you sitting here worried about some irrelevant shit!" she yelled. "I can't believe you. I should have just went and told my daddy."

I knew that was coming. Every time her ass was in a tight spot, she threw her pops in there, and that shit got me all the time. I threw my hands up to calm her down.

"Aight, aight, cool." I was saying it was cool, but in the back of my mind, I wondered why in the hell he was comfortable enough to come to her with that. But it didn't matter; he wouldn't be alive long enough to tell anybody about it. "I'll handle them; don't worry."

"What you mean handle him?"

"Why?"

"Just asking, damn!" she yelled and walked in the bathroom and slammed the door. She was up to something. I would damn sure find out what it was, but right now, my main focus was handling these two muthafuckas. I picked up the phone and called Mello.

"'Sup, Mitch."

"We riding out."

"Say no more," he said and hung up. I grabbed my keys and hit the door. I would deal with Wynn and all her bullshit later.

LAKE

*T*he shit was all fucked up. A nigga was tweeking for real. After Mira got us thrown out of the hospital, I decided to give her a few minutes to calm the hell down. I went back up there, and she had me banned. I couldn't believe that she was that upset that she wouldn't even let me check on her.

I went as far as calling the hospital to see if they would give me the information that I was looking for, but they asked me for some kind of security word that she set into place for people to get information on her. I didn't have the information needed, so I did the next best thing. Desperate times called for desperate measures. I picked up the phone and called Ms. Lori, her mother.

"You got some nerve calling me, nigga," was the first thing out of her mouth when she answered the phone.

Ms. Lori and I had a decent relationship. She made it her business to stay out of our relationship, and I respected that. She told me as long as I kept her daughter safe and out of harm's way, she had nothing to do with it. She said she knew how young people were—together one day and broke up the next. Even when Mira cried to her about our problems, she gave her advice and kept it pushing. She would tell me how she felt about certain shit, but not to the point where it was interfering, and it made things easier for us.

"Things got out of hand. I never meant for it to get to this."

"You damn right this shit out of hand. What have I always told you, Lake?" she asked, but I didn't say anything. "Huh!" she yelled a little louder.

"I know I put her in harm's way, but I didn't know that shit was gon' hap—"

"No, you didn't think you was gon' get caught!" She was mad. I could tell because I could hear her spitting through the phone. "When I said keep my daughter safe, I meant from yo' bitches too."

Ms. Lori ain't never cussed so much as long as I'd known her. She was normally quiet and reserved, but not right now. Honestly, I deserved all this shit and more for what I was putting Mira through. I let her finish cussing me out without interrupting. Everything she said was the truth.

Mira was my backbone. She was there for me through everything good or bad. She had a nigga when I didn't even have my damn self. She never turned her back on me and didn't deserve none of this shit I was out there doing. A nigga felt like shit, and I had to find a way to make this right. I just didn't know how.

"Look, Ma. I'm sorry for putting Mira through this. I don't

know what the fu—what I was thinking." I cleaned up my language a bit because I respected her too much to talk like that. "What I did was dumb, and I'm gon' do whatever I need to do to make this right. I love Mira with all my heart; her and my kids are my everything. I'll never do no shit like this again." She sighed heavily.

I hoped she was hearing me because I meant every word I said. I was done with this shit. A nigga was about to be on the straight and narrow. Miracle was gonna be my only issue. Our relationship was more complicated than anyone knew, but I was gon' have to find a way to make things work. Her and this baby were gonna be an issue; I could feel it.

"I don't know if you can, son." She softened her tone and called me son, so I knew I was breaking her down. "This baby thing got my baby all tore up."

"That baby ain't mine," I lied. I knew it was, but I was gon' have to find a way to deal with that and keep my family. I knew Miracle. She was not about to let me talk her into getting an abortion, but I was gon' try. I cared about shorty, but she wasn't worth my family.

"You don't even sound like you believe that." She chuckled right before I heard the phone go dead.

"Fuck! Fuck! Fuck!" I yelled before I slung my phone across the room. I heard it hit the wall with a thud and then the ground.

I paced the room, trying to think of ways to handle this shit. I needed to have a conversation with Miracle. I just hoped she understood where I was coming from. I could see this going left. I was just hoping that it wouldn't.

Pulling up to the Creek, it had a fucking eerie feeling; you know, the shit that made the hairs on the back of your neck stand up or caused a chill to go down your spine. My eyes scanned the area, but nothing was out of place. Niggas were at the green box serving the fiends, bitches was out half naked, and bad ass kids were running around doing shit they weren't supposed to be doing. I surveyed my surroundings one more time and shook the feeling off. I headed to Miracle's apartment.

I knocked and stood there for a few minutes before knocking again. I opted not to use my key because I wanted her to know that I was serious about the conversation we were about to have. If I just walked in, she would think that things were the same, and they were anything but.

I was about to turn around and walk off, but I heard the locks turn, and she opened the door. My heart sank to my feet. Baby girl looked bad as hell, and it fucked me up because I knew that shit was because of me. I stared at her for a few minutes. Her eyes had bags and were red from crying. Her normally beautiful hair was thrown in a bun on top of her head, and the shit looked matted.

If there was anything that I knew about Miracle, it was that she kept herself up. It was a cold day in hell that she would be caught with a hair out of place. So it fucked me up that I was her hell. I reached out to touch her, and she slapped my hand down and started to cry. I went to console her again, and she tried to shut the door, but I pushed it open.

"Stop, Miracle." I grabbed her, and she broke down in my

arms. "Stop, stop, stop," I said as she started to pound on my chest while I held her.

"I thought you loved me," she squealed, still trying to fight against my hold. "After everything that I've done for you, Lake... after everything." She was breaking me down with every tear, but I was here for a reason.

"You know a nigga care about you; don't ever doubt that."

"You care about me?" she scoffed. I could read between the lines, and I knew exactly what she was referring to, but things weren't as black and white as she would have liked them to be, and she knew it. We were definitely handling some gray shit right now.

"Don't do that, Miracle!"

"You denied our baby?" She looked up at me, and I couldn't answer her because no matter what I said at that moment, it wouldn't come out right. I knew we needed to talk about this baby, but I didn't know if she was in the right mind frame to do so. "Do you even want this baby?"

I didn't know how to answer the question. I didn't feel right about abortions, but it was what I needed to make my family with Mira whole again. I looked into her eyes, and I could see her breaking even more, and I was cussing myself for even putting her in this situation. I was careless, and I was taking full responsibility for it.

"I—I," I opened my mouth and then shut it again. I was trying to find the perfect words to say in such a fucked-up situation. My intentions weren't to come here and argue with her, but as soon as I told her what I thought, it was gonna be a problem.

"I, what?" Her hands found her hips, and I knew right then this conversation was about to go downhill. "What? Let me guess... You want me to get an abortion."

"I mean, think about it, Miracle." I knew I was talking to a brick wall, but I had to try. "Are you really ready for a baby? Let's be for real, and I know I don't want a baby with someone I'm not with."

The last part came out a little harsh, and I didn't mean for it to, but it was the truth, and I didn't know any other way to put it. I needed for her to understand the position that she was putting the both of us in if she went through with this pregnancy. Things were gonna get really hard for me.

"Get out." She pointed toward the door with a new set of tears rolling freely down her beautiful face.

"No, we need to talk about this."

"Nothing to talk about. Your mind's made up and so is mine." She sniffed and dried her face with the back of her hands.

"I mean, let's be real, Miracle. Are you 100 percent sure that the baby is even mine?" I knew the baby was mine, but I was hoping that if she heard my doubts that she would rethink the situation. She picked up the vase that was on the table she was standing by, and she hurled it at me. I ducked to keep from getting hit with it.

"You muthafucka!" She shook her head. The hurt that seeped through her eyes told me that what I said hurt her to the point of no return. "Get out!"

"Listen, I ain't mean that shit. I just—"

"You just what, Lake? Huh? You really wanna do this?" Her

hurt was turning to anger, and that shit could do more harm than good to my current situation. "I mean, if you wanna be real," she mocked me, "I hold all the cards."

I ran my hands down my face because the reality of her words hit me like a ton of bricks. I was indebted to her in a way that kept me from giving my all to Mira, and it was one of the many reasons that I kept coming back to Miracle. Don't get me wrong, I cared about Miracle, but the strings that were attached gave her more pull than my feelings.

"If she only knew." She shook her head and then smirked through her tears.

Something in me snapped, and I rushed her and grabbed her neck and squeezed. I wasn't thinking about anything at the moment; not her or the baby that she was carrying. It was like I blacked out, and when I came to, Miracle was struggling to breathe, so I let go, and she fell to the ground, gasping for air.

"Fuck, Miracle. Baby, I'm sorry. I ain't mean that shit." Remorse slowly crept in my heart. I was fucking up and big time. She didn't even bother to look my way; she just pointed at the door.

"Get out! Get the fuck out!" The pictures shook from the force of her screams. When she finally looked at me, the look in her eyes was one that I had never seen before, and I knew right then that she wasn't the young girl that did whatever I told her to do anymore. She now felt entitled, and she had every right to. I gave her that in more ways than one. "How dare you put your hands on me!" She pointed at me with a shaky finger. "I've been nothing but loyal to you! Oh, you've fucked over the wrong one." She sniffed and tried to walk past me and open the door. I reached out to grab her, and she slapped the shit out of me. "Don't you ever touch me again."

"Yo, I know you mad and all, but if you hit me again, I'ma fuck you up." I knew I was in the wrong for putting my hands on her, but she wasn't about to be slapping me like she didn't already know what the deal was.

"You ain't gon' do shit but keep being the bitch that you are." She snarled her nose. "Now get the fuck out."

"Miracle, don't do nothing—"

"Do what? Tell your precious Mira that you ain't all you're cracked up to be?" She crossed her arms across her chest and rested her weight on one leg. "I hate you!" she said just above a whisper.

"Don't fucking say shit you don't mean, Miracle."

"Fuck you! Get out!"

"You know a nigga got love for you, but shit is just fucked up right now." I tried to reason with her and get her to see things my way. Up until now, I could pretty much tell her what I wanted, and she hung on to every word, but shit was changing before my eyes, and I wasn't feeling it.

"You don't' care about anybody but yourself, Lake. Nobody but yourself." Her words were final, and I knew if I had any chance to get through to her that I would have to give her some space. She was pissed in her own right, and my presence was making the situation worse.

I looked at her one more time and opened the door and backed out of it. The moment I shut the door, I could hear her turning the locks, and the next thing I heard was her wails. The shit was eating me up because I never meant to hurt her the way that I had. I grabbed my head and ran my hands down my face. Never in a million years would I have thought that I would end up here.

Taking the steps one at a time, I slowly descended the stairs. My head was down, so I didn't see what was coming until I heard the shots. *Pow! Pow! Pow!* and then the burning sensation piercing my torso. I grabbed my stomach where the blood started pouring from and stumbled to the ground. The pain that I was feeling was nothing that I had ever felt before.

"Ohhh my god, Lake! Somebody help me!" I could hear Miracle scream right before I heard tires screeching. I tried to lift my head but to no avail. "Baby, please hold on, baby. I'm sorry. I don't hate you. I didn't mean it. Oh God! I didn't mean it!" she cried out. "Please, somebody call 911!"

I felt her warm tears hit my face as I faded in and out of consciousness. The shit was cliché as hell, but I was getting cold. My eyes fluttered, and before I faded all the way out, my eyes met Miracles once more, and the fear that was present hurt me because there was nothing that I could do about it.

"Heart! They shot him! They shot him!" I heard her scream, and I released the tears that I tried to keep at bay. "Mitch! It was Mitch!" she cried, and then everything faded to black.

HEART

$\mathcal{I}$ was sitting in this waiting room waiting for somebody to tell me what the fuck was up with my brother. I was getting impatient, and everybody at the front desk that was up there talking and laughing was about to feel my wrath.

"Oh God, oh God, oh God." Miracle cried and rocked back and forth in the hospital chair. We all tried to console her, and there was nothing that anyone could do to calm her. I felt bad for her because she had to see that shit.

"Fuck this shit!" I yelled and jumped up and headed to the front desk. Lala tried to grab my arm, but I snatched away from her. She knew me, so she didn't take offense to it; she just followed closely behind me. I slammed my hands down on the desk. "Can I get a fucking update on Lake Childs, please."

"Are you immediate family?" the little ugly one with the

fucked up gap in her teeth asked in an attempt to be smart. What she didn't know was she was putting her life in danger with the way I was feeling.

I reached over the counter and grabbed her by her collar and lifted her out of her chair, pulling her so close to me our noses were almost touching.

"I want a fucking update on my brother," I said through gritted teeth while peering at her. Tears welled up in her eyes, but that shit didn't move me. I had been calm long enough, and they were testing my patience.

"Sir, if you don't let her go, I'm going to have to ask you to leave," the other nurse said that was sitting up here doing nothing with the one I had jacked up.

"Do it look like I give a fuck about that?" I looked at her, and she jumped. "I don't know what the fuck I gotta do to get some fucking answers. What the fuck I'm gon' do is shoot this mutha-fucka up if y'all don't tell me something!" I yelled and let go of ol' girl. "Update!"

I felt Lala put her hand on my back, and that calmed me, if only for a moment. I needed that little bit of peace. The nurse started typing something on the computer and then she looked up at me. I could tell that the news that she had wasn't good news because she was afraid to tell me.

"He's in surgery; that's all I can tell you." She rolled her eyes and something in me snapped. I tried to get around to the other side of the desk, but Lala wouldn't let me. She was strong as shit, and when I tried to push her out the way, she slapped me.

"That's enough now, shit. Let's go!" she screamed. I snapped out of my rage and looked down at her. "Heart, baby, let's go!"

The tears that cascaded down her face caused the ones that I was holding onto to fall. I wasn't a nigga that cried often, but this shit was tearing me down. I hated that my nigga was in there going through that shit. Mitch was gonna pay and with his muthafucking life.

Taking her into my arms, I held her while we cried and comforted each other. I didn't give a fuck about who was watching. I ain't never felt no shit like I was feeling right now. Once we got it all out, I took her hand and headed back to the waiting area.

I hated that La and Miracle were fighting right now because they really needed each other, and they were both too stubborn to realize it. When we got back to where we were, Mira was walking up with her mother.

"What the fuck is she doing here!" she screamed and pointed at Miracle. Miracle didn't respond; she just continued to cry and rock in the seat. "Why the fuck is she here?"

Miracle stopped rocking and just peered at Mira. I stepped in between where Mira was standing and where Miracle was sitting. Neither one looked stable, and right now wasn't the time.

"Now ain't the time for this shit. Lake laying up in this bitch and y'all out here worried about the wrong fucking shit. You know what—fuck this shit." I turned to leave, and La grabbed my arm, but I jerked away. She looked me in the eyes and nodded her head. It was like she knew that I needed a minute to get my shit together. I couldn't stay here.

I charged down the hallway and ran right into security that was at the nurse's station that I had just left. The look I gave them made them freeze and refrain from approaching me. A nigga wasn't in the right frame of mind to be dealing with this bullshit. Someone was bound to feel my pain fucking with me.

The elevator was empty, and I needed that. As soon as the doors closed, I screamed to the top of my lungs. Punching the walls a few times helped to ease a little of that frustration that was built up from not knowing what the fuck was going on with Lake.

My Tahoe was right in the first row. I hopped in it and tore out of the parking lot of the hospital. Reaching for the blunt that I had in the ashtray that I stole from Lake caused me to hit my steering wheel a few times.

"I should have fucking been there!" I yelled to myself.

My phone went off, and it was a text from Lala telling me that everything was gonna be okay and that she loved me. I knew that everything she said was true, but right now, my mind was on one thing and one thing only.

Lighting the blunt, I dipped in and out of traffic, heading to Mitch's house. He was gon' see me and soon. I pulled to the red light across from the golf course when I noticed Mitch's candy apple red Cadillac STS in the opposite lane. *Perfect!*

The rage that flowed through my body had me gripping the steering wheel so tight that I rubbed the skin off my palm. I busted a U-turn and came down on the wrong side of the road until I was beside him, and then I rammed the side of his car, causing him to skid off the road, but he regained control of the car and sped up.

Jumping behind him, I floored my Tahoe and caught him in no time. When I got up behind him, I floored it again and hit him so hard his bumper fell off in the road and rolled under my tires, but I didn't stop there. He tried to pass the car that was in front of him, but I hit him, causing him to spin off into the other lane and right into another car.

I pulled over on the shoulder and got out of the car, headed in the direction of Mitch who was trying to get out of the car before I got there. He kept looking in my direction and working his way out of the broken window because I'd smashed his driver's side door.

The moment I got to him, I grabbed him and snatched him the rest of the way out of the car and hit him repeatedly in the face. I reached in the back of my pants for my gun, but I was wrestled to the ground.

"Put your hands behind your back!" the police yelled.

"Fuck!" I yelled out.

They handcuffed me and dragged me to the police car, literally. When they got me to the nearest car, they threw me in the back and shut the door. I could feel my phone going off, I knew that it was Lala I worked myself to a position to be able to twisted my body 'round so that I could get to it.

Once I had my hands on the phone, I hit answer and put it on speaker. "Yo!" My tone was harsh and aggravated, and I was too amped up to try and control the way it came off. Whoever was on the other end was gonna have to take that.

"Baby, where are you?" Lala cried, and I automatically thought the worst.

"What's wrong, La? He alright?" I swallowed hard, preparing myself for what she was about to say. Scared was an understatement, but I needed to know.

"He coded, baby." My heart felt like it stopped. Lake was the only nigga I trusted in all this; he couldn't leave this world. If my nigga died, I swear the town of Mooresville was about to feel my pain. "He's on life support."

"What the fuck does that mean!" I didn't mean to yell at her, but I wasn't in a position to control my emotions.

"He's not breathing on his own right now; the machine is doing it for him, but they did a CAT scan, and he has brain activity, so that's a good thing." When she said that, I felt a little relief but not much. "I need you to get back up here, baby. Mira and Miracle acting crazy, and the hospital wanna put them out. I can't take this... not by myself. I need you," she cried.

"I can't come right now, baby."

"What you mean, Heart? Where are you?"

"I'm in the back of a police car, and they taking me to jail. Call my lawyer, and I'll try and call you later, aight."

"Wait, what? Baby, no, what happened?" she asked, but right as I was about to answer, the police yanked the door open and started asking me a bunch of questions about what happened. I could hear Lala screaming on the other end of the line, and I couldn't tell if she was upset about what just happened or if something had happened at the hospital. I prayed it wasn't the latter.

I made sure to make eye contact with Mitch before the police car pulled off. I wanted him to know that this was far from over, and before it was all said and done, he would be resting in a pine box.

MIRA

*A*fter they told me that he coded, I didn't know what to do. I had to walk off. The pain of knowing that I may not ever see him again mixed with being in the same room with the woman who was claiming to be pregnant by him, was slowly killing me. I was becoming physically sick. Even though he said that he wasn't the father, her dedication to being by his side through all of this told me otherwise.

The way she broke down had me thinking other thoughts, so to get myself together, I walked off. I needed to get some fresh air. My mind was on the wrong thing at the moment, and it wasn't fair to be thinking about any of that while Lake laid in there fighting for his life.

Most women wouldn't even be here after the bullshit that I had been through with him lately, but here I was. I wasn't even 100 percent, but I was here making sure that he was okay. That's how much I loved him, even through him making a fool out of me.

I had faith that he would wake up from this, and when he did, he was gon' have a hell of a lot of explaining to do. I wanted to know what I did so wrong to make him treat me this way. I was everything to this man and a good mother to his kids. What else did he need? I knew that him cheating wasn't my fault, but I couldn't help but to wonder what didn't I do. What could I have done better to keep this man at home.

Why was I feeling like this? I knew I was a good woman, and any man would have been happy to have me, but I just couldn't figure out for the life of me why the man that I loved didn't treat me as such.

I sat down on the bench that was in the smoking area of the hospital and just cried until I couldn't cry anymore. I wanted to hate him so bad, but I didn't. I was starting to feel like the woman that I vowed I never would be. The ones that sat around and allowed their men to cheat and take them back because they loved them. I didn't want that to be me; I wouldn't let it be me. I was worth more than that. I just couldn't leave him alone right now. He needed me to be there by his side so he could make it out of this.

"What's a pretty lady like you doing out here all alone and crying?" I looked up into the perfect set of bedroom eyes. Despite the cuts and bruises on his face, he was fine as hell. He was tall, and you could tell that he was mature. I had to shift positions in my chair to try and control my clit from throbbing. The man had the power to control my body without even touching me; we hadn't even had a conversation yet.

I shot him a smile and then put my head down. I didn't feel right sitting here flirting with this man while the father of my children was upstairs on life support.

After a few minutes of uncomfortable silence, I finally got up and started toward the hospital entrance to clear my head of all nasty thoughts that I was having of this beautiful stranger.

"Hey!" He stopped me as I was about to walk in. I wanted to keep going and ignore the handsome stranger, but my body betrayed me, and reluctantly, I turned around to look at him. "What's ya name? You at least have to tell me your name." When he smiled, the hairs on my arm stood up, and I could hear my heart beating out of control. No matter how hard I tried to calm down, I couldn't. This man was trouble.

"Mira." I smiled back unintentionally.

"Nice to meet you, Mira." He licked his lips, and without my permission, my most prized possession started to leak. I clenched my legs together to stop the madness. "I'm Mitch."

Without saying another word, I nodded my head and headed in the direction of the hospital. Once I reached the doors, I took off running toward the elevators. No man had ever made me feel like that—not even Lake—and it scared me.

There was no way that I was about to let another man make me feel the way Lake was making me feel right now, and the way I just acted in front of that man showed me that that was exactly what would happen.

When I got back to the waiting area, Miracle was still there, and that pissed me off. My mom was keeping me sane while she was here, but she had to leave to get my kids, so it was just me, her, La, and my feelings about this whole situation.

I walked over and took a seat right in front of her. I needed her to give me the answers that Lake couldn't right now. I needed to know why she thought this was his baby. I had every intention on being civil with this hoe, but the way she looked at me threw all of that out the window.

"Why the fuck are you here?" I yelled at her, and she glared back at me like I was the one that was in the wrong. Her demeanor was confident, like she knew that she was the one that was meant to be by his side through all of this. "You heard what the fuck I said?"

"I deserve to be here just as much as you do." Her tone was calm, but there was power behind her words, and I was eager to know where it came from, so I challenged her.

"Bitch, you're nothing but a side bitch. You do know that, right? He used you when we weren't getting along." I gave her a dose of reality. I didn't know what Lake told this girl to make her feel the way she felt, but she stood strong in her truth; too bad it wasn't real. "What, he fucked you a couple of times and you lucked up and got knocked up with a baby that he doesn't even want or believe is his?"

My words bothered her, I could tell. Her eyes twitched when I said it, but she was not about to let me know that, so instead of flipping, she calmly crossed her legs and swept the long strand of hair that fell out of the messy bun that was on top of her head.

"Oh, is that what he told you?"

"It ain't like that, baby. You know that baby ain't mine. I would never do no shit like that to you." I tried my best to mimic Lake. It was an epic fail, but she caught my drift.

"He and I both know that ain't true, and in the back of your mind, so do you. I think he was just trying to spare your feelings like I'm trying to do." Sitting back in her chair, she crossed her arms and glowered at me like she knew something I didn't.

"So you're one of them, huh?" I scoffed. "One of the delusional ones that make up whole relationships in your mind off a sample of the dick." I chuckled, but I didn't believe the words that came out of my mouth no more than she did. This girl was too comfortable for her to just be a fling. I had a feeling she was about to tell me just how close she was with my man.

"That's just the thing; I didn't sample the dick. It's mine and has been for the last two years. Lake is more mine than he ever was yours." She smirked.

I did exactly what I said I wasn't going to do... I lost it. I stood up and punched her right in the mouth. She countered and hit me back with a two piece. She was quick with her hands, I would give her that because I never even saw it coming. We were going blow for blow until I felt myself being pushed back. I thought I was getting jumped, but then I heard Lala's voice, and I stopped.

"Y'all two chill the fuck out! Lake in that fucking hospital bed fighting for his life, and Heart is sitting in somebody's fucking jail right now, and y'all doing this?" The tears that cascaded down her face broke my heart, but I was too angry to show her any sympathy. I just wanted her to move out of my way so that I could get my hands on this bitch. "Both of y'all should be ashamed of yourselves."

We both just stood there like raging bulls, ready to attack. Neither of us addressed what Lala had just said; we were just that pissed off. I loved La, but she didn't know what the fuck I was feeling at this moment. She wasn't going through what I was going through, so she didn't have the right to tell me to calm down.

"I don't even know why the fuck you're here," Miracle said to me. "I know if my man's side piece put me in the hospital, I wouldn't be."

Her words stung, but I would never give her the satisfaction of seeing me sweat. She was right about one thing; I didn't know why I was here. Even though shit between me and Lake are fucked up, I couldn't imagine myself not being here for him at a time like this.

"I didn't know side bitches had an opinion."

"I'm far from a side bitch, bitch!"

"Are y'all fucking serious!" La screamed to the top of her lungs. "Just stop! Lake lied to the both of you. If you gon' be mad at anybody, be mad at him! You can't do that though, 'cause he is laying in there, and we don't even know if he gon' make it, and y'all worried about who he fucked more." Her eyes darted back and forth between me and Miracle. "Got damn!"

Before I could tell her how I felt about the situation, the door to the back opened, and Dr. Smire walked out. I turned my attention to him, praying that he was about to tell us something good, but the way he was looking told me otherwise.

"Dr. Smire." I stepped forward and waited for him to speak.

"It's touch and go right now. He's still on the ventilator, but like I explained before, there is brain activity. I need to know if things go south, who will be making the decision whether or not to keep him on life support?"

"What do you mean if things go south?" Miracle stepped up. "You have to save him," she cried.

"I will be making the decisions." I rolled my eyes in her direction and focused my attention on the doctor. "I'm his fiancée and the mother of his kids; he doesn't have any family. He grew up in the foster system."

"No, she won't be making any decisions." Miracle started fumbling around in her bag. "I will." She pulled out a piece of paper.

"No! What she is about to do is get the hell on away from here. She's not wanted! If Lake was woke, he would tell you that she is no one to him!" I yelled in her direction. I was tired of this girl, and she just kept coming like it was her duty.

"What's your name and your relationship to the patient?" Dr. Smire asked, completely ignoring my outburst. Miracle handed him the folded-up piece of paper. Lala and I looked at each other and then back at her.

"My name is Miracle Childs and I'm his wife!"

ALSO BY NIKKI BROWN

Catalog

Messiah and Reign 1-3

I Won't Play A Fool For You (Messiah and Reign spinoff)

My Love And His Loyalty 1-3

I Deserve your love 1-3

Bury My Heart 1-2

Beautiful Mistake 1-3

Beautiful Revenge

Riding Hard For A Thug 1-3

You're The Cure To The Pain He Caused

Key To The Heart Of A Boss 1-3

I Got Love For A Carolina Hustla 1-3

A Hood Love Like No Other

CPSIA information can be obtained
at www.ICGtesting.com
Printed in the USA
LVHW031411020619
619874LV00002B/366/P